C-M

by KEITH HOLLIHAN

ChiZine Publications

FIRST EDITION

Distributed in Canada by
HarperCollins Canada Ltd.
1995 Markham Road
Scarborough, ON M1B 5M8
Toll Free: 1-800-387-0117
e-mail: hcorder@harpercollins.com

Distributed in the U.S. by
Diamond Book Distributors
1966 Greenspring Drive
Timonium, MD 21093
Phone: 1-410-560-7100 x826
e-mail: books@diamondbookdistributors.com

Library and Archives Canada Cataloguing in Publication

Hollihan, Keith
[Novels. Selections]
Gamification / Keith Hollihan.

A flip book.
Issued in print and electronic formats.
ISBN 978-1-77148-151-9 (pbk.).--ISBN 978-1-77148-152-6 (pdf)

I. Title. II. Title: C-monkeys.

PS8615.O4376G36 2013 C813'.6 C2013-905163-5
C2013-905165-1

CHIZINE PUBLICATIONS
Toronto, Canada
www.chizinepub.com
info@chizinepub.com

Edited and copyedited by Brett Savory
Proofread by Samantha Beiko & Kelsi Morris

Canada Council for the Arts Conseil des arts du Canada

We acknowledge the support of the Canada Council for the Arts which last year invested $20.1 million in writing and publishing throughout Canada.

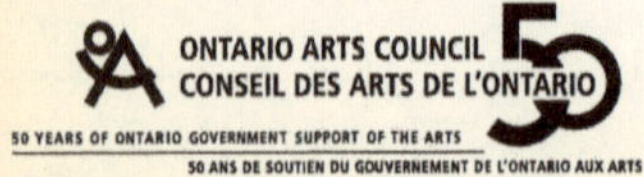

Published with the generous assistance of the Ontario Arts Council.

Printed in Canada

C-MONKEYS

". . . one man's fact is another man's fiction."

—L. Ron Hubbard

1

"I wish you were right," he said, "but our decline will be faster than you can even imagine. Even so, your ignorance puts you in good company with world leaders, captains of industry, and esteemed economists. I hope that will comfort you when the last drop drips and human civilization comes to an end."

It was December 3, 1973. We were talking about oil and the latest Mideast strife they were calling the Yom Kippur War, the OPEC embargo, the way the markets had been rocked and how the threats and violence were spreading over the planet like a viscous and uncontained spill. It was the sort of leisurely and speculative conversation you can have at length when you are far from actual troubles and have few pressing worries, and the weather is tropical but with a pleasant breeze and there is plenty of shade from the fierce sun. We were on an island sixty miles off the coast of Singapore, an exclusive health clinic for the wealthy. My conversation partner, Dr. Harold Braunhut, was a heart patient and geologist. He must have been a brilliant one. Apparently, the organization he worked for, an energy conglomerate he declined to name, had deemed him important enough to keep alive at no small cost.

I laughed at Braunhut for calling me foolish. Though a bit sharp-tongued and impatient, he had a good-natured disposition. I'd met other brilliant people before and they were often bitter misanthropes through and through without a shred of hope for humankind. I got the feeling that Braunhut was all the sadder because he wished he was less brilliant and more wrong.

"Why is it so hopeless?" I asked dryly. "Can't we dig deeper or use less oil? Can't we find other energy sources? We're a very resourceful species when our backs are against the wall, don't you think?"

I was provoking him in a friendly way. Braunhut leaned forward, his face reddening with enthusiasm for the argument, then leaned back just as quickly. A nurse had entered the palm-shaded courtyard. They came and went often. Checking vitals. Administering medications. Occasionally adjusting a straw or applying a dab of zinc oxide to prevent a prominent nose from getting too much sun. This nurse was a tall redhead named Amber. Braunhut fancied her. We all had our favourites, and a few that we ducked whenever possible.

Braunhut resumed his argument in a calmer, less agitated manner because he knew that Nurse Amber would prescribe a cold sponge bath if she even suspected his blood pressure had become elevated.

"There are no more sources," he said. "None that can be tapped by conventional technology. The downward spiral can't be stopped unless—" he hesitated and I waited. "Unless we seek a new source that's beyond our reach. That's—"

Nurse Amber, in her sweet way, stopped him cold.

"I have messages for both of you," she announced in a honeyed voice. "You have a telex from America, Mr. Wells."

She handed me a sealed envelope and gave a flash of sly smile.

"And you, Dr. Braunhut, I have an order from Dr. Ostler. He'd like to perform your physical and do a new set of blood work. You haven't done anything naughty like sipped some coffee or nibbled a croissant this morning, have you?"

Braunhut grinned with the attention. "I can promise you, Miss Amber, I adhere to my strict diet at all times because of your watchful eye."

"If only all our patients were as agreeable as you, Dr. Braunhut, I wouldn't know what to do with my free time."

"You should spend it on the beach, suntanning," Braunhut suggested.

"With my complexion, doctor, I need to be very careful of the sun. Follow me, please."

"I'll be right with you."

Neither Braunhut nor I moved. It was always a pleasure to watch her walk away in her short nurse's uniform.

"This is it," Braunhut muttered. He looked anxious suddenly, alert.

"What is it?" I asked.

"If my check-up goes well, I aim to leave tonight. I must. I have an important business conference to attend, the most important of my life. Do you know I haven't even met my new colleagues yet? We are about to launch a great venture, one that may change the world, and I'm stuck here, helpless. I swear to you, Gadsen, I wouldn't miss this if my life depended on it."

"In America?" I asked, fishing for more information. "That's quite a distance for a meeting." It seemed in poor taste to let the comment about his life depending on anything hang for too long. I focused instead on the impracticality of lengthy travel, no matter how urgent.

But Braunhut shook his head. "Wish me luck."

I raised my glass in that spirit, and watched him go. Alone, I tore open the envelope to read my telex. The message was one I had been waiting for, and the information it relayed was very interesting indeed.

There were approximately thirty patients in the complex, to the best of my knowledge, though I sometimes wondered how many more were incapacitated or hidden from us because they were famous and needed extra privacy. I was only interested in Braunhut, and we spent a good portion of every day together, timing our meals and even our exercises. We were about the same age and both American, outnumbered by the Europeans and Arabs. I was educated and sophisticated enough to hold my own with him. I know an unusual amount about many different subjects, and have the quiet confidence to project even deeper knowledge. This has put me in good company many times before.

Braunhut was sullen when I first met him, at the fruit buffet one afternoon, fretful, as if deeply worried about complicated matters. Sitting at the next table over, our light meals eaten, I made an off-hand comment about longing for a Chesterfield cigarette and it was enough to break through his sombre mood.

"Chesterfields are my favourite brand of cigarette," he said. "I prefer Kings. You?"

It turned out we had pledged at the same fraternal organization, that we both preferred Bebop over the Beach Boys, that our favourite guilty pleasure was a Manhattan with a spike of single malt scotch, and that we missed a few other luxuries our current physical conditions had put out of reach, perhaps for the rest of our lives. I did not disclose my own ailment but implied that it was daunting and unpleasant and not readily cured by surgery or drugs. There were a few strict rules about the resort—namely that you put all of your mental and physical energies on the business of healing and did not talk about your illness or your work. So, naturally, most residents talked of nothing but. Braunhut found my life interesting enough. I had been a dime store hack throughout my twenties and thirties, had written hundreds of pulp novels, and Braunhut asked me to tell him the plots of this and that, as a way of passing the time. I told him about the assassination of the African dictator to secure a supply of uranium, and about the troop of American soldiers trapped in an Italian insane asylum besieged by a Panzer battalion, and the plot by a pharmaceutical giant to contaminate the water system with hallucinotropic drugs in order to influence a presidential election. Soon, he unloaded the burden of his worries on me, which concerned the problem of oil and how to get more of it. He'd worked for academic institutions and a half dozen corporations and a few governments to do his part to secure the world's most important dwindling resource, but had found no organization or institution with the vision or the ingenuity to accomplish anything meaningful with sufficient urgency. Until, that is, he was approached by an organization he would not name.

"It doesn't matter who they are," he told me. "What matters is there's a chance. And I should be working on the problem with them right now, and I would be if it wasn't for this damn heart."

He'd been hired by registered letter, had never even spoken with his new colleagues on the phone, but a sizable cheque had been deposited in his account, a year's salary merely as a goodwill bonus, and he had been informed discreetly by an academic colleague that the money and the organization were legitimate, and that it was the chance of a lifetime. So he'd resigned his position, but in the urgency of closing out his affairs and handing off his research, he taxed himself too hard and collapsed. When he awoke in the hospital, he was told that he was lucky to be alive, and that there was nothing that could be done for him but rest. He despaired in his room for two days before he was visited by a lawyer from a prestigious firm on the East Coast, who assured him that his new employer still wished to honour his contract, and had in fact arranged that he be sent by airplane to the most advanced treatment centre in the world, at company expense, in order to hasten his recovery. Braunhut agreed, of course, and soon, in spite of his own doctors' protests, he was airlifted and flown across the continent and over the Pacific.

"And I woke up in this paradise, which is just a damn prison."

"A prison?" I asked. "Why do you say that?"

"Because I want to leave, and they won't let me. Have you noticed that the wall, though pleasantly covered in vines, is thirty feet high, and has barbed wire and broken glass up top? Have you noticed that whenever we want to place a call, it takes days to book and something always goes wrong with the connection?"

"No," I laughed. "I hadn't noticed, except to feel relieved to be cut off from the world. Braunhut, you're being ridiculous. The wall is to keep people out, not in. You and I are ordinary men, but you can imagine the anxiety that some of the truly wealthy and privileged feel about locals. If this is a prison, we're very well-treated prisoners."

"Maybe prison is not the right word. Institution, perhaps. I only know that I want to go and they won't let me."

"Because you're sick. You were nearly done for when you came here. They're looking after you, Braunhut. You should be grateful."

"I'm grateful enough. But you don't understand what's at stake. The consequences."

"You need to relax," I said. "The more stressed you become, the further your goal recedes."

It was one of the mottos of the place, written in cursive above the entrance to the beach-side lecture hall.

"I wish I had your capacity for blissful ignorance, Gadsen," he said. "Nothing bothers you!"

I smiled and did not try to convince him

otherwise, though of course, it was not true. My worry was Braunhut and the organization that had hired him.

I lay in the darkness on the bed in my private quarters, unable to sleep. A square of brilliant moon shone through my window and projected itself like a film onto the wall next to the bed. Somewhere in the room, unseen, a gecko quacked, an abrupt squeak of protest I knew greatly outsized the little beast that had produced it. There was no other sound, not even the rustle of a breeze through the palm fronds until there came a soft scuff, a hesitation outside, and then the door handle turning. Our doors did not have locks—privacy was an unnecessary luxury where health emergencies were concerned—but I steeled myself in anticipation of whatever ill intent had come visiting. Then I heard a whisper.

"Mr. Wells?"

I recognized the voice and propped myself up in the bed on my elbows to invite Nurse Amber in.

"It's Dr. Braunhut," she said.

I planted my feet on the cool floor.

"Is he gone?"

I wished I'd been there. There were questions I would have asked, and I had hoped that Braunhut, if he knew the end was near, might have answered them.

"Not gone," Nurse Amber said. "Leaving. He's asked me to get you so that he could say goodbye."

"At this time of night?"

Her whisper went even softer. "He's not leaving with physician approval."

I stood. I was dressed only in pyjama bottoms, my torso bare. By the light of the moon through the open door I could see her face clearly, sombre, guilt-ridden, intent.

"You're helping him escape," I announced.

"A girl has to eat," she said.

"I expect he's paying you better than that."

I stripped without asking for privacy.

Nurse Amber was in her uniform. I wore the clothes I would wear for a walk on the beach, light trousers and a shirt made from a beige, hempish cotton that did not cling to the skin and yet shielded the intensity of the sun. We hurried through the compound for the gate. Two men stepped from the shadows as we approached: Braunhut and an orderly with a poorly shaved jaw and a thuggish, threatening demeanour.

"Thank you, Gadsen, for seeing me off. I would've hated leaving without a goodbye."

I did not know what to say. He was intent upon going and yet he also seemed reluctant to leave.

"It's nice of you not to depart without telling me."

"I wish I'd told you more," Braunhut said. "But I was afraid you were a journalist in pursuit of a story. I wish I'd trusted you sooner."

I shrugged as if to say, I wish you had, too.

"We must leave now," his thuggish companion interrupted.

Braunhut looked helpless.

"I'll go with you to the airport," I said. "You have a plane waiting?"

"I've hired one and a pilot."

"And a nurse, apparently."

"She insisted on coming once she discovered my plans. I'm grateful."

"Our very own Florence Nightingale," I said.

Nurse Amber shot me an angry look as she squeezed by.

"Take two," she said to Braunhut, opening a bottle of pills.

She sat between us in the back seat. The road was paved but in poor condition and we passed over potholes at an inadvisable speed. Braunhut seemed distressed by the commotion and the urgency.

"Why don't you slow down," I said to the driver, but Braunhut told the driver to go faster.

"We must hurry," he said.

The road was empty of traffic and there was no danger from oncoming cars.

"It's your plane," I said. "It won't leave without you."

But Braunhut had gone silent again.

"What is it that you wanted to tell me?" I was getting tired of this game.

"This meeting that I'm going to," he began. "It's not in America."

"I'd assumed as much," I said. There was no time for him to travel that distance.

"I'm flying six hundred miles," Braunhut said, "to an uncharted archipelago between Borneo and Tahiti."

"An unusual place for a meeting," I said. "If it's uncharted, how will you find it?"

"I have coordinates," he said. "They were given to me in code."

"A secret meeting on a secret island. What other surprises have you got for me?"

"It's a gathering of scientists, engineers, and managers. All of us employed by Chopek Energy."

"You mean Dr. Petr Chopek?" I said.

"You've heard of him?"

Braunhut looked at me across Nurse Amber's chest. She was doing her best to ignore our conversation, staring straight ahead, as though anxious about the speed we were travelling.

"A brilliant petrochemical engineer in his youth," I said. "Today, the fourteenth wealthiest man in the world. He'll sell his drilling assets and expertise to anyone, including the Soviets, the East Germans, and even the Red Chinese."

"And the Americans, and the French, and the Argentineans. It's not that he has no political scruples, it's that he sees us all as equally bad actors on the world stage. He's post-nation. He's pan civilization."

"A nice way of saying that he is that new breed of global businessman who believes in the liquidity of capital and the primacy of profit."

Braunhut nodded. "I suppose you're right, but I'd rather believe in his noble intentions."

"And what is the great Chopek up to?" I asked with sarcasm.

"To the best of my understanding," Braunhut said, "Chopek has developed technology for undersea drilling at depths far beyond any we have been capable of reaching before. He has discovered new Saudi Arabias, new Libyas, new Iraqs beneath the oceans. Not only will this replenish global reserves for centuries to come, but it will wrest power from the terrorist states of the Middle East and make the kind of conflict we are seeing today pointless. As a friend of Zion, I can only be thankful. As a human being, I'm ecstatic. We have not yet fought wars over oil, but that day is almost here. The strife, the death, the inevitable collapse of civilization as our sources run out—all of that can be avoided because of Chopek's advances. I need to contribute in any way possible, even if it means my life."

I nodded. "I understand," I said. "I value my own life more highly than you do yours, but I can appreciate and admire the sacrifice you are willing to make for the rest of us. Are you sure it's necessary, though? You say he has many scientists in his employment? Not to question your stature, Braunhut, but does he really need one more?"

"He is, from what I understand, in most desperate need of leaders in my relatively obscure field of paleogeology."

"And, remembering that I am foolish and ignorant, why would a paleogeologist be essential to his work?"

"Because Chopek is drilling at depths we do not understand except by extrapolating what we do know about the tectonic plates and substratum of the planet from pre-Cambrian times. The terrain and conditions below the ocean floor resemble nothing we would encounter on the surface, not since the age of dinosaurs."

Our road had approached the coast again and became bordered on one side by a high chain-link fence. When the fence ran out, the driver steered the vehicle through the opening and onto smoother pavement. A runway. I saw a plane in the dimness of early dawn, sizable but squat, nose raised proudly, broad tail low to the ground, a Douglas DC-3. It was probably thirty or forty years old, but they were reliable aircraft, still used as island hoppers in the South Pacific. As our car approached, a weak light appeared in the cockpit, and a quack emitted from the fuselage as the electrical systems fired on. We pulled up to the tail of the aircraft and parked a respectable twenty feet away, then the driver hopped out of the car and opened the door for Braunhut. The propellers of the plane began to chop and turn before erupting into a low droning buzz saw. Nurse Amber slid along the seat to exit from Braunhut's door. I followed awkwardly, ducking my head to extend my body out. When I looked up I saw a gun pointing at my face.

The orderly stood in front of me, his hand gripping Braunhut's collar. Nurse Amber was cringing fearfully and leaning against the car as if to move as far as possible from the threatening cannon. Braunhut's face, even in the dim light, was ashen.

"Out," the orderly said, flicking the gun in emphasis.

I extracted myself slowly and stood next to the nurse.

"You don't need to harm them," Braunhut said, no doubt sensing the finality of the threat. "It's me you want. They're innocent."

"And unwelcome," the orderly said. "And unlucky." He raised the gun with clear intent.

The door of the plane cabin popped open, the pilot appeared in the entrance and lowered an aluminum ladder, which he then hooked on the edge to brace it tight to the plane. He stopped in his crouch when he saw us, shocked by the scene below.

My forearm parried the orderly's arm as he pulled the trigger and the bullet screamed askance. The pilot, in jumping up from the shot, hit his head against the edge of the fuselage and began to windmill his arms. Balance lost, he plummeted from the cabin, not even grazing the ladder. At the same moment, Braunhut collapsed in the orderly's grip as though the bullet had struck him, though it had not. I drove the heel of my hand into the orderly's jaw and chopped his wrist so hard that his fingers became momentarily useless and the gun dangled from his hand. Then I threw myself into his chest.

He was much bigger than me. Though taken by the surprise of my attack, he responded quickly. We rolled on the ground, and I struggled for advantage. It had been a mistake to engage him in such direct combat but I feared the gun and what he would do with it when strength returned to his grip. I searched for the gun now, blindly feeling about the ground with one free hand, as his choke hold began to do its work. When he suddenly released the clench I felt a rush of life-giving air screaming into my lungs and saw Nurse Amber standing before us. She had both hands on the gun and was pointing it at the orderly's chest. I extracted myself and wriggled away.

Gasping, I could hear a distant sound of police

sirens and wondered if the cavalry were coming to rescue or apprehend us. I had a feeling it was the latter. Braunhut sat awkwardly on the ground but whispered that he was okay, that he had only fainted, but that we must flee. I assessed the situation. The orderly's arms were lifted in surrender. I wondered about the condition of the pilot.

"Watch him and don't let him move," I said to Nurse Amber as I rose.

Her eyes were locked on the orderly's eyes and her stance was wide in that way that amateurs have when they brace themselves intensely to shoot.

She did so. The cannon blast obliterated all other sound.

When I blinked again, post-explosion, I saw Nurse Amber still in her shooting stance, the gun out before her, the orderly lying flat on his back, a gaping hole in his chest filling with red. She opened her mouth and yelped in shock.

"Oh, no!"

"Give me that," I said, and tore the gun from her hand.

I hauled Braunhut to his feet by his shoulders and braced him against the car. Then I ran to the airplane. The pilot still lay where he had fallen on the tarmac, his eyes open, his neck twisted to an unnatural angle.

"He's dead," I called over the buzz of the propeller.

I ran back to them, and looped Braunhut's arm over my shoulder.

"Oh, God!" he groaned. "I'll never get there now."

"Do you still wish to go?" I asked.

"I must! But how?"

"Get his belongings," I said to Nurse Amber. "His briefcase especially."

I dragged Braunhut to the plane and up each narrow step, careful to keep him in balance. When we were in, I sat him down in the first seat and turned about. Nurse Amber was coming up the ladder behind me, faster than I had expected. She handed me Braunhut's briefcase, then reached back for his suitcase and lifted it up without effort, though it was hefty. We could still hear the sirens, even over the roar of the propellers. I saw blue and red lights strobing, the cars racing along the outer fence.

"What are you going to do?" Braunhut asked. His face was beaded with sweat.

"Fly us out of here," I answered.

"You're a pilot?" Nurse Amber asked.

"One of my hidden talents," I said.

I scrambled to the cockpit and checked the fuel gauge and electrical controls. The police cars were rounding the fence.

Nurse Amber appeared at my shoulder.

"I've closed the cabin door," she said. "We're clear for take-off."

"You don't need to come," I said. "It's your last chance to stay."

She shook her head, barely interested in my question, and peered out the window at the cars pulling up to the plane.

"He won't live without me. If you take the grass

runway, behind the control tower, they'll need to chase us."

There were police standing on the tarmac now, their guns drawn, pointed at the girth of the plane. In the propeller wind their hair and jackets blew chaotically about.

It was a sound plan. I engaged the stick and nudged us forward and around.

"Look after Braunhut," I commanded.

By the time I had rounded the control tower and aligned the nose along a grass runway, shots were ringing out. I tensed, waiting for a bullet to penetrate the cockpit windshield or the fuel tank. I saw a car racing up the tarmac to try to swing around and intercept on the grass. I leaned forward and brought the engine into full throttle. We would see if it could fly.

Bouncing, jostling, picking up speed. The grass runway looked smooth but it was not. The plane rattled uncontrollably as though breaking up. The end of the runway neared, our speed still too low. A police car appeared but remained off to the side, without blocking our way, as though the driver knew we would have to pull up short. I thought of Braunhut and what he was willing to chance and rammed the throttle forward even as I pulled back on the stick. The runway ended and we passed beyond the edge of the cliff. The plane wavered and sank. Our weight pulled us down toward the rocks and the water. We almost skimmed the surface before we began to climb. Then we lifted, and kept lifting, and topped the height of the cliff behind us and lifted some more. We soared on. The sun had broken the surface of the horizon ahead, and I adjusted the wings in salute.

2

The DC-3 is inefficient and complex but this works in its favour. The failure of even a few parts rarely leads to the catastrophic failure of the system as a whole. But like any lovingly wired and patiently soldered jalopy, it reaches that point where the lurching starts, and great snorts of exhaust shoot from its engines, and the miracle of flight seems like a dubious proposition at best.

We were bleeding fuel. A slow trickle that made a mockery of the flight plan, set by the coordinates Braunhut had whispered to Nurse Amber before unconsciousness overtook him. I'd feared a nick to the line, a penetration of the tank, so many stray bullets had flown toward us. My fear was not disappointed. The electrical system became erratic, the gauges occasionally jumped readings, and the fuel load felt lighter than it registered. I could sense imminent failure in the engine, the drone increasingly hoarse.

It was for this reason that I could not leave the controls, let alone the cockpit, to see to my friend, Braunhut. It was for this reason that I was not with him when his breathing became irregular, his pulse weakened, his chest stopped moving, and he succumbed. Nurse Amber appeared in the doorway. There was no more need for urgency and vigilance. She clung to the doorframe and then collapsed in the co-pilot's seat, and told me that he was gone.

I did not nod or give her a glance. I merely steered.

The silence went on. We stared at the endless blue before us. Finally, she asked me what I intended to do.

"I intend to survive, if we're lucky. We passed the point of no return a while back and I'm not certain we'll be able to reach our destination. It'll be close and rough. I'm losing ability to manipulate our pitch and yaw."

"Our what?"

"Our attitude. How we adjust the wings to bring her in on a safe angle of attack."

"To attack what?"

"To attack a landing strip. To land. Safely. On a runway."

"We're going to crash?"

"We need to prepare for that," I said. "Fortunately, the ocean is the biggest runway in the world, so I'm not likely to miss it. And the swells look relatively calm. At least from up here.

She looked down, then back at me, then buckled her harness.

"Can you send out some sort of distress signal?"

I shook my head. "This aircraft's stripped. No distress. No identification marks. No manifest. We're in a black ops plane. I wouldn't be surprised if there were bales of cannabis under the floor."

"I don't understand."

"I don't either. Except that Dr. Braunhut, or his employer, was very concerned about covering his traces."

"But why? And why would that orderly have pulled a gun on us?"

"Your guess is as good as mine."

She clenched my forearm.

"Please tell me we'll make it," she said.

"Okay," I said. "We'll make it."

I finally saw a speck in the distance that could have been land.

"There," I pointed.

She sat up. She squinted. Then she saw it.

A lonely russet-coloured peak. It grew in size, rising from the horizon like a shark's tooth. As a place of safe landing, it did not look promising, steep and jagged-edged. But we could not be choosy. Landing on the water anywhere near land was the best I might be able to manage.

I imagined that we looked lonely in the sky. We were lurching. We were coughing and sputtering.

"Braunhut said the island was part of an archipelago," I said above the growing engine noise. "But I don't want to chance it by trying to go around that peak to see what's on the other side. I'll take us down as close to the island as I can get. If you're conscious after we crash, free yourself from the harness and swim for the hatch. Don't worry about me. There'll be no time to waste. If you're trapped in the cabin, you'll probably find a bubble of air but with our weight, we'll sink fast."

"Oh, Gadsen," she said.

"I hope you brought zinc oxide for our beach holiday," I said.

I altered our pitch, eased the throttle, and tried to bring us in as softly as possible. The surface screamed up to meet us. A thousand feet, five hundred, two hundred, fifty.

We hit.

For a moment, I thought I was paralyzed. I could feel an intense pressure on the back of my neck and nothing more. Then I realized I was floating, my limbs rising, though my torso was still pinned to the seat. I opened my eyes. There was water up to my neck, a violent churn of bubbles that made it difficult to see. The cockpit window had caved in. I remembered, now, how I had dipped at the last second and the water had smashed through the nose, flinging me back with the collision. I plunged my hand below the surface and struggled for the release on my chest harness. My hand grasped it, twisted it, but could not free the catch. The water rose above my mouth. I fought the panic and felt more deliberately for the clip. It snapped open and I shrugged my way out.

The cockpit was angling downward. I could not see Nurse Amber. I took a last breath of air and turned myself around to enter the cabin.

It was still within, almost peaceful. Fragments of the fuselage leaned this way and that. A seat cushion floated gently by me. Then I saw a body, arms and legs akimbo, hair delicately spread out, eyes closed, mouth open, and knew it was Braunhut. I pushed past him and he bounced slowly against the wall. The old DC-3 had cracked its spine. I took a last look for Nurse Amber and squeezed myself through the split in the fuselage, escaping into the expanse of ocean depths. I had done enough scuba diving to know that orientation can be nearly impossible in some circumstances. Was I looking up or down? I saw light in both directions, a faint greenish glow. So I released a swallow of air from my mouth and watched the trail of bubbles crawl to the surface. I swam after that trail, wriggling, stroking, pulling my way up. The whole way, it felt as though I were descending into the depths, and I needed to fight the irrational urge to turn around and swim the other way.

I popped up in a slick of fuel, viscous and globular, breathing hard until I could recover. I twisted around to search for the island. I saw the russet-coloured peak. I looked about for Nurse Amber again, and called for her, my throat sore, my voice hoarse. Even my hearing was off. It seemed blocked and I could make out only muffled sounds. I lifted myself out of the water as high as I could and scanned around. Nothing except more debris, patches of flame. I did not know the extent of my injuries and I could not judge how far I would need to swim. It was time for me to try and make it.

Whatever energy I had left was stolen from me in that struggle for shore. I am a strong swimmer, but the current held me back. I was bewildered at first, and then I realized that I was caught in a rip tide, one of the most vicious I'd ever experienced. I floated for a moment, ceasing my struggle, and tried to determine which direction the current was coming from, then I angled myself off from it, and headed for the far corner of the island, hoping that this time I could accomplish some distance and pull myself in.

Closer to shore, the waves finally worked for me and I felt myself lifted dangerously up. I saw massive boulders ahead, and very little space between them, water crashing through like the churn of tailings in some vicious drill bit. I stopped swimming and tried to position myself so that my legs were in front of me, wide apart, and bent. I soared forward on the next wave and plummeted down to a boulder, as formidable as a skyscraper wall, though I managed to plant my feet against it and soften the jarring collision as one does during a parachute drop. Pressed against its surface now, I clung to the jagged protrusions and bobbed beside it, ducking whenever successive waves came crashing in. I inched my way along and timed my passage between boulders until I could begin to stand. I was even more cautious once I could lift my body up from the water. A sudden wave might cut my legs out. A smashed skull or broken leg would be the end of me.

But I did not trip or smash, I emerged from the boulders and stumbled across the looser rocks and up onto a kelp-covered plateau and collapsed on its flat surface.

My head felt clear. There was no damage to my

body. I was exhausted beyond any weariness I had ever felt, but unscathed. It seemed a miracle. When I stood, I had a moment in which my balance did not feel quite right, but the moment passed. I walked cautiously across the kelp to the edge and hopped down. The beach was covered in sharp iron-coloured rocks that gave way to pebbles and a fringe of sand.

I saw a gleam of white or silver farther down the beach. Nurse Amber? I scrambled faster, tumbling once, fearful of twisting an ankle but anxious to cover the distance.

When I arrived I saw that she lay mostly on her side on another flat plateau of rock, one knee bent, chin delicately tilted, eyes closed. Her nurse's uniform had been torn and draped her like two halves of an open curtain. Beneath the uniform her skin was caramel coloured, streaked with strands of dark sea weed. Her bra and panties were a deep red, like a bikini. I knelt beside her and reached for her neck, fearing the worst. When I touched her skin her eyes fluttered and she turned onto her back. She saw me and a horrified gasp came from her throat. I pressed my hand to her face to calm her. She grabbed my hand with a ferocious grip and then seemed to come to her senses.

"Gadsen," she said.

"You're alright," I answered. "We made it."

"I had a horrifying dream," she said.

I could believe it.

Nurse Amber was in good condition, though sore. I helped her walk to the fringe of sand. We sat and looked out at the ocean. Other than pieces of wreckage along the rocks, there was nothing left of our plane. If a rescue flight were even looking for us, there would be little for them to see.

"What do we do?" she asked.

"For now, the essentials. Food. Fire, if we can manage it. Water, if we're lucky."

"How?"

"Food will be easiest," I said. "In those tidal pools, there's bound to be shellfish, starfish, jellyfish, crabs. We can gather them up and make a terrific meal, add some seaweed for Vitamin C and D. Fire, I can make, if we can find some driftwood, since there doesn't seem to be any vegetation. With a bit of flint, some dried kelp, and a piece of cloth, I'll have us going in no time. Water will be a challenge. It looks lifeless here, and I'm not sure I want to venture far from the beach until morning. But hopefully we'll find a pool that isn't too stagnant. We might get lucky and have a storm within a few days. We'll need to stay warm, though. At night, it will be cooler than you might expect."

Her dress was useless and would not even cover her now. I had lost my shirt somehow and wore only my light cotton trousers, stained grey and black. Neither of us had shoes.

"What kind of writer are you?" she asked as though suddenly angry. "You fly a huge plane like you've been a pilot all your life. You know how to survive when shipwrecked on an inhospitable island. You karate chop a man with a gun and wrestle him to the ground."

A man you shot point blank, I thought but did not say. Not every nurse could manage that.

"I like to write from what I know," I explained. "So I do as much hands-on research as possible to lend my stories verisimilitude. I've mountain climbed and scuba dived. I've raced dog sleds across the Arctic and fired most weapons. You should be thankful I'm so well rounded."

"I am thankful."

I pointed to the ocean. "I'm thankful you made it to shore somehow," I said. "You were unconscious the whole time?"

She shook her head. "I'm not sure. I remember the crash. And then I remember floating. I felt as though the water lifted me like a flower and placed me on that flat rock."

"Amazing," I said. I thought of how I'd needed to crawl out of the sinking plane, and how the rip tide had almost drowned me.

"So many rocks," she said. "And Dr. Braunhut didn't live to see them. I wonder if any are worth studying."

She threw one. It struck a larger rock and ricocheted into the nearest tidal pool with a hollow splash.

"Why would Braunhut have cared about these rocks?" I asked.

"Because he was a geologist. That means he studied rocks, right?"

"Ancient rocks," I said. "But no, he wasn't a paleogeologist."

"What do you mean?"

"That telex I received yesterday was from my lawyer in New York. He made some discreet inquiries on my behalf."

"So?"

"So Dr. Braunhut didn't study ancient rocks."

I stood up. It was time to gather sea food.

"What did he study, then?" she asked.

"He was a paleozoologist. He studied ancient animals."

I left her to puzzle what I did not yet understand myself. Why Braunhut had lied, and what he had really come here to do.

We ate well, better than I promised. The tidal pools were our fish market. The crab meat was among the juiciest I'd ever tasted. Giant raw oysters, pried open with a sharp bit of flint, the insides filled with fleshy meat and delicious brine. The mollusks I roasted on hot coals until they opened like treasure chests. The sea urchin was as soft as a pat of melted butter. Nurse Amber did not want to try it at first, but my moan of pleasure was so convincing she scooped out some with her fingers and could not restrain her own delight. I cut up jellyfish and tossed it with dried seaweed for a salad that would have made the chef at 21 jealous. If only we'd had a chilled bottle of 1957 Chablis to wash it down.

The darkness came. The waves seemed less urgent in their crashing against the shore, the foam of each crest glowing with fluorescent sparkles. The full moon rose, a brilliant silver planet. A hundred million stars in the blackness; so many shooting stars we stopped calling out whenever we saw one.

I saw a shape, low to the ground, moving up the rocks.

I stood, my rock knife gripped firmly in one fist, and grabbed my driftwood torch wrapped in cloth and lit it in the fire to step forward and peer more closely.

"What is it?" Amber whispered.

I did not answer right away.

"I don't know," I said, finally. "A seal, maybe. A trick of the light."

I saw no other movement. I did not want to alarm Amber more than necessary, so I sat back down on the sand beside her, though I could not relax again.

"I can't believe what we've been through," she said. "It almost seems like three lifetimes in one day."

"At least. You need sleep," I said.

"You need sleep, too."

"I want to keep the fire going."

We lay on the sand, a few feet apart. I sensed, correctly, that Nurse Amber was too demure to accept the inevitably of our need to share body heat. But in the middle of the night, I felt her roll into me, and fit herself into the wrap of my protective arms.

3

I awoke before her, alarmed to have been so solidly asleep. My muscles had tightened painfully. My lips were dry. I pulled my arm gently out from underneath her torso, sat up, and added some more dried and spongy wood to the fire to rekindle it. After I had it going again, a soft wisp of smoke rising, I left her and relieved myself behind a boulder, then found a tidal pool, splashed my face with bracing water, and searched under beds of kelp for sleeping crabs and oysters. It was another bounteous harvest.

We ate quietly, as though we had accepted the futility of vocalizing our worry.

"I'm thirsty," she said.

I nodded. "We need to find a supply of water today. That's our primary goal."

I did not add that if we could not find water, we would need to consider more desperate plans to survive.

"This island," she shuddered. "It's horrible."

"It feels like we've landed on Mars, doesn't it."

From the sky it had appeared as though the peak had taken up most of the island, but it looked to be a mile from us on shore, and it would not be an easy walk. We would be prone to turned ankles, skinned knees, cut palms.

"Sometimes the lee side of a mountain can be a very different terrain," I said, with as much optimism as I could muster. "I'll find us some walking sticks to help with our balance."

It wasn't difficult to find two good sticks of driftwood, knotty and twisted, but as smooth as polished stone. They made us feel stronger and more capable, as good tools should.

We walked the sand for some time, searching for any sign of an easier path, such as a dry creek bed, that would help us walk across the craggy rock. I finally found a bed of more crumbled rock, porous like unrefined ore, and guessed that a run-off of water had once coursed through here. It was not a good sign that the ground was so dry, but the ore-like rock was peculiar. It seemed almost volcanic. I wondered if it had been a recent eruption, and whether that explained why the landscape up to the peak was one burn-like scar.

We walked along the creek bed, treading carefully to avoid sharp rocks. A cut foot would be another disaster. Infection. An inability to move quickly. Fever. A clumsy amputation or worse. We made slow progress. I waited for her often, and kept my senses alert to any dangers.

It was amazing how parched we both felt in such a landscape, unsheltered from the sun. Our bodies were not dehydrated, far from it, and yet we longed for water. I guessed that the salt we'd ingested with our meals contributed to the deplenishment.

We saw the cliff rising and soon we were upon it. The rock was the same volcanic ore as the dry creek bed, and the cliff itself was like a plume of black smoke that had solidified on its way skyward, like an underwater explosion in the early days of the Earth's formation.

"Hold this," I said, and passed Nurse Amber my walking stick.

I tested the rock face. There were plenty of toe and finger holds, though the rock was sharper than I would have liked and more prone to crumbling. I climbed thirty feet, like a crab clambering upward, but did not see what I had hoped to find, a hollow in the rock that might have collected rain, any sign of wetness.

I made my way down, and hopped the last ten feet to the ground.

"We need to get to the other side," I said.

Nurse Amber looked doubtful, anxious.

"I'm afraid of heights and I've never rock climbed before."

It would have been our quickest way but I had anticipated her reluctance to try. Her bare feet and thighs, her wrists. She would probably have cut herself to ribbons on the way up.

"It doesn't matter," I said. "We'll find a way around on foot."

I was doubtful about this. The cliff face looked like a natural wall vivisecting the island.

We made our way northward. Sometimes the easiest path took us very close to the wall; at other points, we needed to scramble over rocks and away from the face before clambering back up. There was soil on some of the flatter, more sheltered patches of ground, but very little vegetation beyond sparse grass. I became lost in thought as I walked on, debating how close we might have made it to Braunhut's coordinates, whether the air speed had been accurate. We'd flown for three hours and forty-seven minutes before losing altitude. Had it been enough?

I heard Nurse Amber cry out. I whirled even as she seemed to slide from my sight, as though pulled into the earth. When I reached her and grasped her hand and hauled her back up, we realized that she had merely stepped in a spot that I had avoided by chance. What had seemed like solid ground was actually a hollow covered in loose rock and dirt that collapsed under her weight. An animal's den probably, though we had seen no sign of animal life yet. I kept my stick at the ready and poked into the hole. After discovering nothing threatening, I began to dig with my hands to widen the entrance until I could view what was below. The space she had fallen into was a smooth bowl, a natural formation that was perfectly dry, almost like a giant hip socket minus the joint.

"I'd like to see this more closely," I said, and hopped down before she could protest. The depth was to the top of my head. If she'd fallen she might have broken both legs. We would need to be more cautious.

Crouched within the bowl, I sensed a brush of

cool air. I allowed my eyes to adjust to the semi-dark and examine the wall more closely. The stone surface was remarkably smooth. It was not as cold to the touch as I would have expected, merely pleasant. I traced my fingers along it aimlessly and then felt something, a seam, a crack. I ran my finger along the seam and traced a circle, like a rounded mirror or a plug. This could not be natural. I pushed, and felt as though I were pushing a mountain. I pried my fingers into the seam of the circle from both sides at once and pulled. Out popped a round cork of rock and a rush of escaped air. I fell back, the rock still in my hands. I couldn't have been more astonished.

"What is it?" Amber called.

The cork of rock was as large as my chest. It should have weighed more than I could possibly have hefted, but it was as light as cork, too, as though porous within. More like bone or dried sponge than stone. The entrance was wide enough to crawl through and wider still within. We would be able to stand, it seemed. The tunnel itself was as round as though it had been bored, and yet it looked natural rather than man-made. I knew that volcanic rock could have a strange mix of properties, driven up as it was from miles beneath the Earth's crust. I had encountered something as soft as limestone and as smooth as polished quartz.

"I believe I've found a short cut," I said, and popped up to grin at her.

Perhaps if we had been less desperate, she might have questioned my proposal more sceptically.

The tunnel was tall, but we needed to hunch. The rounded floor made walking even more difficult. It was dry, for the most part, but every slick spot, every patch of powdery sand, set us awkwardly reaching out for the walls to brace ourselves from falling. The breeze made a persistent *hush*, as though the mountain were warning us to be quiet. We had no light, but though we quickly lost the glow of the outdoors behind us, we needed nothing in the way of illumination to maintain our vision. Perhaps it was merely that we had become used to the dark, but I suspected there was a faint fluorescent property to the polished quartz that somehow enhanced the optics of our surroundings. The passage was not completely straight. It did not "bore" directly through the mountain. Its shifts were organic, however, without any sudden angles or sharpened turns. It proceeded like a tunnel that a mole might have made, intent on a destination but leisurely, digging through a particularly spongy patch of ground.

And then the ground seemed to flatten and broaden even as the tunnel expanded in girth, and I sensed a slight incline. I stood straight. Amber did the same. The quality of the rock changed, too, a sandstone that was warmer to the touch, drier, grittier, and it felt also as though the world had opened to different sounds—our own scuffs, some sense of a larger world. With each step, the light brightened, too, until I stopped because we could see a line of sunlight cutting across the floor in front of us.

Nurse Amber's hands were on my back and she

peered beyond my shoulder, sharing my trepidation and hope. I had never seen natural light so delineated, so physical. I plunged into it as though it were water. My stride grew in boldness. Then, I stopped again. We stood at the mouth of the cave, and before us was another world.

The colours were overwhelming at first. There was the intense blue of the sky overhead, wisped with stray white clouds. There was a whiteness to the powdered sand before us—it stretched to the edge of the water and along the shore in both directions endlessly with none of the harsh jagged rock of our old beach. There was the shape of the bay, which had a caldera-like perfection and the colour of the water within it—a transparent turquoise, edging at depth toward teal. And finally there was the verdant green of a ring of four other islands surrounding the bay.

Despite the magical beauty of this place we had found, perhaps one of the most stunning locales I had ever visited in the world, I was drawn to the sight of the boat making its way across the water to the beach where we stood.

A large war canoe with a single mast and an unfurled sail. I saw three paddlers, with one man standing at the prow, like Washington crossing the Delaware. There was no point in hiding, if there was even a reason to hide. They were heading directly toward us.

I waved, not frantically but as a signal. The man in the prow lifted his hand in acknowledgement. He was a white man, dressed in a shirt with collar and pants. His companions appeared to be natives.

By their dark skin and sinewy leanness, I guessed that they were racially akin to the aboriginals of Micronesia.

"I feel uneasy," Nurse Amber said.

I understood what she meant. We should have bounded in joy and hailed our rescuers, yet I could not help but wonder what sort of outpost we had discovered.

"I'll look after you," I said.

She followed me onto the sand.

We waited at the water's edge for the war canoe. With surprising velocity and force, it wedged its way onto shore. The man at the prow leaped into the water in sandals. His clothes were more rugged than they'd seemed from a distance, his face weathered and lined, like an experienced outdoorsman. He greeted me with a cautious, almost suspicious nod, and handed a canvas water canteen to Nurse Amber.

Nurse Amber didn't hesitate but tipped it above her mouth and drank. When she was finished I drank, too, and found the water wonderful, thick, replenishing. I wiped the back of my hand across my mouth.

"Dr. Braunhut?" the man asked.

What could I do but answer yes?

4

We sat on the gunwale and had a view of our own island receding and our destination drawing closer. The aboriginals ignored us. Our lack of clothing was of no interest to them. They attended to the task of paddling with discretion and vigour. The water was even more remarkable up close, the turquoise so light in hue and the sun so penetrating a force that we could see dozens of feet below the surface, sometimes to the dazzling coral formations that grew skyward like a flower garden.

Our rescuer's name was Troch, but he said to call him Hans.

"Only my father is called Troch, or sometimes Captain. Me, I'm Hans."

"Your father was a sea captain?" Nurse Amber asked.

Troch tried not to look at her, in her red panties and bra, acting the gentleman beneath the gruff exterior.

"Cargo ships mostly, some whalers, a frigate or two, all around the Orient, from the time when you needed to know these waters and bays like your own hand, where to shelter when the typhoons came, where to find materials if you needed repairs or supplies, which islands to avoid. Headhunters and cannibals everywhere, then. These boys here might not know what human flesh tastes like, but I bet their mums and dads did."

Nurse Amber shuddered. I had a thought.

"Did your father discover this bay?" I asked.

But Hans only grunted, as if he felt he'd said too much. I wondered if there was a safe way in for a large ship, or whether the rocks and the strange current would keep everything out, effectively sealing us off from the outside world. Did that explain the strange microclimate?

"You have a Dutch accent," I said instead, trying to probe for more information in a congenial way.

Hans grunted. "Never been to the Nederlands, but yes, old Captain Troch is Dutch. We were Java people until the war. My mother was Filipino, but she passed in one of them Jap camps. Your plane crashed, yeah?"

"Yeah," I said. "We almost didn't make it. We were lucky."

If they'd seen the plane going down, why had they not sent out a rescue team earlier? Even as I opened my mouth to ask, Nurse Amber screamed and scampered back in her seat, pressing into the back of one of the aboriginals in her fear.

We were all startled by her outburst.

"Kappa," one said, and all of them grinned, showing toothy smiles of pleasure.

I flinched, too, when I saw it. A reptile, about the

size of a cat, and with a similar grace and lightness in its movements. It must have clung to the side of the boat at some point across the harbour, and now it climbed in and curled about Hans's leg. It was not scaly or jowly like an iguana, though it had a similarly elongated tail, but smooth-fleshed and broad-skulled like a frog, with stubby arms and legs, and even stubbier fingers and toes. Its colour was a mottled green, but even as I thought this, it seemed to change in the sunlight or the air, its skin losing some sheen of wetness to become a light purple dotted with orange specks.

"Ach," Hans said. "Kappa ain't nothing. No danger," he said to Nurse Amber as if in apology, then reached down and stroked the top of the creature's skull with two fingers. The thing responded by pushing up and arching its long throat, flaring its mouth at the far corners as though about to hiss.

"These islands," Hans added. "They're lousy with lizards."

We were met on the dock by a short man of about forty dressed in a pressed summer suit with a necktie. He thanked Hans for delivering us, and shook my hand warmly.

"Dr. Braunhut, I'm so glad to finally meet you in person. I'm Hilden, the director of personnel."

I did not want to dwell long on our presumed relationship, so I introduced Nurse Amber promptly.

"As you know," I said, "I've had health issues, and the clinic thought it best if I were accompanied by a trained medical nurse."

"We were not expecting another guest, but we are more than prepared to make Nurse Amber welcome. We will get you clothes and food right away, and you will have amenities for bathing. I'll arrange adjoining rooms, if that is acceptable, so that Nurse Amber may see to your health."

I wondered, with his smile, whether he doubted my innocent explanation and was implying something improper. I looked to Nurse Amber and she nodded. She seemed more concerned about being separated than about her reputation.

"Thank you," she said, meekly.

I looked around. The beach gave way to a plaza of smooth grey stone, highly polished like a rock that had been through a tumbler. The buildings that surrounded the plaza were also smooth, and all of the entrances, window casements, and arches were rounded. The ground inclined and I could see stone bungalows stacked up the slope of a hill, as in certain mountain towns in Greece. What sort of place was this?

Before I could ask another question, Hilden interrupted me.

"The conference begins shortly," he said, "with a speech by Dr. Chopek and an afternoon social. If you are well enough, and feel up for the gathering, we will help you get ready. Of course, Nurse Amber, you are most welcome to join us, though I don't think the more academic discussions will be of much interest. Whatever we can do to make your stay more pleasant, please let any of the staff know."

"I will," Nurse Amber said. "You're very kind."

"That sounds perfect, Mr. Hilden," I said. "Would you mind bringing us to our rooms now so that we can rest?"

"This way, please," Hilden said, and gestured for us to cross the plaza and take the path below the large arch.

"This stone," I said, "is it volcanic rock?"

Hilden nodded with enthusiasm. "Incredible material. Light. Easy to shape and work with. And it filters all our drinking water. The purest water you've ever tasted. Everything you will find here has been developed from local materials and substances. Gutta-percha. Palm oil. Copper. Rubber. Nitrogen. Dr. Chopek is a genius at making the most of what the earth and the sea has to offer, and turning it toward productive uses. But you'll learn all about that soon."

"And your energy source?" I asked. "How do you power your complex, run your machinery?"

A hesitation, followed quickly by a laugh. "You're testing me, Dr. Braunhut. You want me to sound like a fool among experts." He wagged a finger. "I won't do it. You'll be with your colleagues soon enough and you can all share a laugh at my expense then."

I smiled in return but my question had seemed innocent enough until that moment.

The lush vegetation was well-pruned in the vicinity of the buildings, the dense green interspersed with colourful flowers of unusual varieties and extraordinary size. There was a sense of paradise about the place, a calm abundance. Each room, it turned out, was its own separate bungalow.

As promised, Nurse Amber and I were situated in neighbouring bungalows, a short walk apart. We entered her bungalow first, and Hilden described its features as he opened closet doors, filled a glass of water, and turned back the corner of the sheet on the queen-sized bed within.

"Hot and cold running water, volcanically filtered and delicious. These slots at the top of each wall are for airflow. You'll find it cool in here during even the hottest days. There are clothes in the closet you should feel free to use, mostly Malay and Japanese, in style. If they're not to your taste, please let us know. Among the toiletries you'll find several exotic creams, scrubs, wraps, sponges, and exfoliants, all made from local substances and materials. We leave you to your privacy."

She nodded her thanks, and looked exhausted. I did not share her fatigue. Hilden and I went on alone on the short walk to my own bungalow.

"I'm so glad you were able to make it," he said. "And your health seems much better than we had even hoped. You've lost weight?"

"About thirty pounds," I said, thinking of Braunhut's approximate size. "The diet in the health centre was strict. The company has been extremely generous and understanding."

"The company is Dr. Chopek, and it's all for the greater good," Hilden said. He opened my door. "I won't see you in. Our conference begins in thirty-nine minutes from now. Despite our relaxed surroundings we are very punctual. If you are unable to join us because you are too tired, you will be missed but everyone will understand."

"I'm not particularly tired," I said. "Would it be possible to see Dr. Chopek before the conference? I would love to express my gratitude to him personally."

"That's not necessary," Hilden answered firmly. "Dr. Chopek spares little energy for formalities, but he will call on you when he has need."

"I understand," I said, and thanked Hilden for his welcome. Then I stepped into the room and closed the door politely behind me.

I was wary and suspicious, but I was not immune to the seduction of a hot shower. The stall was in a tub of volcanic rock. I looked closely at the polished, mottled surface—something drawing my attention—and noticed a small gecko-sized lizard on the bottom, a miniature version of the creature that Troch had called a kappa. Its colouration matched the grey-black within. Was the creature even alive? I reached down to touch it with my finger and saw it blink, though it did not stir, even as I got close. I pressed my finger into its skin and was surprised at how moist that skin felt, how pliant, and how willing the creature was to suffer my violation. After a few minutes of study, I stood up and found a tooth brush to brush my teeth—the paste unusually salty and gritty. Then, without thinking, I turned back to the shower and turned on the tap. The water misted more than it flowed, but it was surprisingly hot and I drew my arm back to adjust the temperature. Too late, I remembered the creature and looked down. It was difficult to spot because of its colouration, but then I saw it, taking the spray full on. Why hadn't it fled from the heat? Only when I stepped into the shower basin and my foot landed next to the lizard did it disappear, fitting itself through the drain and sliding away.

To my surprise, the insubstantial power of the misty shower was more than sufficient to soak me, and between the heat and whatever minerals it contained, I felt as though the dirt, my tiredness, my muscle aches, and even my anxiety and malaise were massaged thoroughly, the combined tension of those forces released from my body and mind.

Weariness was beginning to press on me, but I found some food on the kitchen table, some caviar of excellent quality, an unleavened bread, some more sea urchin and a plate of whole sardines, along with a bowl laden with starfruit and durian. It was a meal fit for a king. I ate all of it, even smearing the remains of the caviar up with my finger.

After I ate, I searched for clothes. My own pants, on the bathroom floor, looked like rags that had been used to clean a chimney. In the closet there were other loose pyjama-like pants and colourful long shirts in the Southeast Asian style, and also a selection of kimonos. There were only light slippers for footwear, nothing I could use to traverse sharp volcanic rock. I put on pants and a shirt, and tried one of the kimonos. My slippers fit perfectly and made me feel surprisingly agile as if there was a springiness to the step and a grip to the sole.

According to the clock on the wall, I had only ten

minutes before the meeting. I had hoped to poke my nose into places it didn't belong, to mingle with people who were not staff but outsiders like myself, but there was no time. I decided to call on Nurse Amber instead.

Her door was shut. I knocked. I called out her name. I peered into the window but could see nothing past the bamboo slats. Finally, I stepped back to the door, and though it made me feel like a thief or a pervert to do so, I opened it up.

She lay on the bed, naked, without cover from a sheet. I froze in my step but Nurse Amber did not stir. I called her name again and saw no movement. I stepped closer and finally reached her side. I saw that her back—her beautiful flawless skin—was moving ever so slightly. She was breathing. I touched the side of her face, preparing myself for a shriek of embarrassment when she awoke, but she did not stir. I pressed my fingers against her neck to take her pulse. It was strong enough, and the air was shooting from her nostrils with the heaviness of her sleep. Best to let her continue sleeping, I decided.

Outside, I contemplated my next move. It was not difficult to guess where the meeting was taking place. Every bungalow had disgorged a guest or a couple, relaxed and tanned, who were walking casually now down the sloped paths that were winding together like streams forging a larger river. I fell in among them. I nodded and smiled when appropriate, but I allowed myself to appear lost in thought, as though I were in a reflective state of mind and desired to be alone.

We funnelled into a large building and entered a grand hallway, the lines of the building futuristic. It was necessary to duck at first because the ceiling was so low, but the height overhead grew like a wave expanding in all dimensions at once, a smooth and organic growth that seemed beyond the protractors of any architect to devise. The space within was perfectly lit, a soft illumination that reminded me of tropical water when scuba diving close to the surface, as though light itself had become, once again, a tactile presence rather than an intangible ray. I noticed in the smoothness of the roof high above my head, a series of what might have been slits, almost like the scales of a fish or the membrane of its gills, through which the light seemed to be passing. The only conventional thing about the space were the rows and rows of chairs. They looked incongruously clumsy and industrially manufactured. I wanted to walk close to the wall, or where the wall and ceiling met on the low slope of our entrance, and touch it, to test whether it was the same volcanic rock as my shower stall, or the hollow Nurse Amber had stumbled into on the other island, but I did not want to draw attention.

I sat in the middle of the auditorium, three seats in from the aisle, between a Caucasian woman with Asiatic eyes whom I assumed must have been Russian or Hungarian, and a tall, regal, bearded man with a turban. I nodded at the Sikh respectfully, making note of the hilt of his ceremonial dagger, and I offered a smile to my Russian companion but received an icy lift of the chin in return. She crossed her formidably long legs and shifted away from me.

We did not wait long. Music began, its source indefinable or coming from every direction at once, vibrating in my body. I could see no organ pipes along the walls to give the sound such force. As the music paused and began again, I was conscious of how odd it sounded, how inhuman in every sense. It was beautiful, but not of this world, though not quite alien to it, either. The lights at the front of the great hall seemed to brighten gradually even as the lights in our seating area dimmed. The effect was magnetic and all of our eyes focused on a man who had appeared on the stage. Dr. Petr Chopek? No, it was Hilden, the director of personnel. By the size of his body compared to the size of the stage, I realized that the space between us was immense. The music dropped in volume until it became a single drawn-out note, then disappeared. A polite but enthusiastic clapping began in the audience.

"Welcome!" Hilden shouted. The acoustics carried his voice to every corner of the room.

"You have travelled far, from all over the world. Welcome!"

Amazingly, a map of the world appeared behind him, projected onto the wall.

"We have citizens from thirty-nine nations gathered here today. Venezuela, India, Saudi Arabia, Iraq, Iran, Turkey, Japan, the People's Republic of China, North and South Korea, Malaysia, Indonesia, Libya, Brazil, Mexico, Norway, the Soviet Union, Canada, the United States of America, Nigeria, Great Britain . . ."

With the name of each nation, a section of the

map illuminated to great applause and wonder.

"But more than being citizens of these great nations, you are citizens of this great planet!"

The applause grew louder, and I saw smiles and nods, more glances of kinship.

"And as citizens of this planet, you are also extraordinary contributors to the advancement of industry, society, and the human race."

Except for me, I thought, *in the guise of Dr. Braunhut, a world expert on the obscure field of paleozoology. What was I doing among them?*

"And why have you gathered here on this Eden of an island, in the middle of the South Pacific, at the behest of our host, Dr. Petr Chopek?"

He waited.

"Why indeed? I will cede the stage to Dr. Chopek so that he may answer for himself."

The applause became deafening, but no one appeared onstage. Instead, the projection of the world map disappeared and was replaced by the image of a thin though healthy-looking senior, seated in an office chair with a broad window behind him and an ocean view that could only have been from our island. A Technicolor likeness. He smiled grandly and waved for us to cease cheering. It seemed as though he were responding naturally to what was taking place in the grand hall. Could it be a live transmission? I had not known such a thing was possible. Why hadn't he come to join us in person? Was his time that precious? He took off his thick glasses, a signal that he was about to begin to speak seriously. The room hushed in response.

"Why are you here?" he asked.

I could not have suggested a better place to start.

"You are here because you are the most brilliant minds in your fields, the greatest gathering of energy researchers, engineers, scientists, investors, and managers the world has ever seen. You are here because the world is in need of your collective brilliance as never before. The time has passed when we can solve our largest problems as individuals. Once, yes, it was possible, and individuals have been responsible for our greatest progress as a species, but the problems of tomorrow are collective problems, beyond the scope of single minds, beyond the scope of isolated computers, beyond the resources of companies in competition with other companies, except those that recognize the power of harnessing all resources at once."

He smiled, and the smile erupted a cheer.

"I am devoting all of my resources to this project, all of my own capital is at the disposal of you, you brilliant few. So what is this problem that we aim to solve together? It is nothing less than the energy future of the planet."

A graph appeared on the screen. Years since the late 1800s, over fuel production, with a line tracing proven oil reserves.

"This is the truth that no world leader will acknowledge. Our insatiable need for energy began, like a gnawing hunger, with the start of the industrial revolution. The simple shift from an agrarian- to a machine-driven world transformed us. We stepped away from millennia of existence tied to the soil. We became free as a result, free in numbers never before known to humanity. This freedom catalyzed greatness. We became free to create, to build, to think, to be. We became freed from the slavery of subsistence. But in the process, the industrial revolution tethered us to another master—energy, primarily crude oil. Our consumption of that complex hydrocarbon has grown by multiples every year since the industrial revolution spread from England and America around the planet. The rate of that consumption is growing steeper and steeper every day, even as two-thirds of the global population remains rural and non-industrialized. We can't get it out of the ground fast enough to physically run the world.

"Why should we fear this wonderful addiction? Because, my friends, we have seen the depletion of our reserves growing rapidly, as well. It began forty years after the industrial revolution, and its force in our history has been nefarious and unseen, like an impending doom, like a monster lurking below the surface of our understanding. And this monster, this doom, is eating up our reserves and destroying our future. They would have you think that the sands of the Middle East contain limitless reserves of oil. Do not believe them. As happened in the American south and west, as happened in Mexico and Venezuela, and in the North Sea, those reserves are becoming alarmingly low. They ask when we will reach the peak of known reserves, and they write about the question in the responsible newspapers and magazines, because we have had a conflict in the Middle East that threatens our reliable flow, but

I tell you we have already passed the peak, though we don't know it yet. We are blind to the erosion of our civilization and our future, because we simply lack the data to know what has already happened. I tell you that our society, our civilization, is already dying. It simply does not know the fatal diagnosis."

A sombre hush. We waited for more.

"And that is why for the past two decades I have poured all of my knowledge and research, all of the resources of my business and my own mind, into determining how we can solve this problem. And I have finally done so. Here on this island, after my long search, I have combined two technologies, one natural, and one very much man-made, to discover how to extract vast sums of oil that have been out of our reach until now."

The image changed again. We saw an interconnected set of continents on a map, but they were shapes unseen on Earth.

"Does anyone recognize these land masses?"

He waited.

"I did not think so. I would not expect so. Unless you have lived your life under the ocean, you would not know the shape and contour of the world beneath the surface. But when the image shifts you see the degree to which reality is limited by perception. Below the oceans is another world, a world even richer in resources than the surface world, a world where exploration and exploitation is encumbered only by the limitations of our technology, our capital, and our imagination."

Next, we saw a vertical cross-section of the crust

of these new continents, and a bed of rock holding a field of oil.

"How do we discover oil in the conventional manner on the surface? Ladies and gentlemen, you of all people know the embarrassing truth. For all of our science and technology, for all of our inductive reasoning, the honest answer is that we guess. We throw darts at a great dart board and we then pull out the darts and peer inside and sometimes we see a glimmer of black within, or the hole itself spits out a spray of it like the plume of some sperm whale, and we know then that there's oil. So we come back with bigger darts and trucks and pipes and ships and we drill drill drill until we can suck up all of the stuff that we guess must be down there—never knowing, of course, whether the field is an elephant or a mouse, whether we have extracted all of it or only a portion. But this is the way we have helped humanity with its hunger. The best guessers among us have become incredibly rich. I say this to you because I have been a very good guesser. I have discovered a few of the largest fields ever exploited, and I have looked like a genius doing it, but I know the truth, that I took some theories and some facts and blended them together and out of that alchemical mixture I turned a hunch into black gold.

"There are few wildcatters like myself still going at it. Why is that? Because there's no profit in guessing anymore. So we have turned to corporations with their vast resources and their research departments, to hedge and fund our guesses. In the process, we've lost the humility of knowing that we were guessing all along. We come up with excuses whenever a drill site doesn't produce. But the real problem is that all the elephants are gone. Or at least, all on the surface of the planet are gone. Those that lurk below the seas are another matter.

"Once, we hunted giant whales across these oceans in our hunger for oil. We set off in ships in search of needles in haystacks, except that the haystack was vaster than any that could be found on Earth, and the needles moved. It was a kind of magic, don't you think? When we found our prize, a great battle ensued, and in the aftermath of the gore and grisly death, the slaughter began. Those ships became floating refineries, harvesting the giant whales then and there, eking out every drop of oil, purifying it, putting it into casks graded by quality, letting the remains of the carcass slide into the deep.

"Though this arrangement was rife with conflict, it represented our first attempt to work in concert with nature in order to secure our energy needs. Of course, being humans we did not understand the notion of balance and we slaughtered as many whales as we could find, destroying the ability of that great animal to replenish itself and renew. We did not husband, we hunted.

"It is time now to turn back to the sea. The difficulty of drilling under the sea is the problem of guessing, compounded many times over. If we guess on land, the cost and difficulty is expensive but not so overwhelming, not impossible. But the cost of guessing below the surface is insanely prohibitive.

Imagine, however, that we did not need to guess but knew where to drill, exactly. What would that make possible? In such a case, the technological costs and even the difficulties would be offset by the tremendous profit. Who among us would not bet a million dollars if we knew, without any shadow of doubt, that we could turn the investment into a hundred million dollars? Every business person, every entrepreneur, nearly every scientist and even a few politicians would be smart enough to sign up for that kind of return."

The image returned to Chopek, his smile benevolent, perhaps mischievous. A lizard appeared on his desk, something liquid in the way it travelled the short distance over the lacquer wood, matching the mottled colour as though pouring itself onto the surface. The smile on Chopek's face grew broader.

"You have by now noticed that we are not alone on this island. Beyond the usual specimens of the tropics, this particular archipelago is home to a singular species of salamander. The natives of this region, from the Seychelles to Malaysia to Tahiti, to the Cook and Easter Islands, all the way to Shanghai and Japan, call this salamander kappa. In some etymologies the word translates loosely as *fire devil*." He scratched at its chin, tickling the little beast, and it rolled over like a ferret with a slithering litheness to expose its underbelly for more touches. "As you can see these are no devils at all, but playful creatures of unusual intelligence for a cold-blooded species. I call them sea monkeys because they remind me of primates. They are as at ease in the sea, among the seaweed and the coral, as capuchins and lemurs are in the branches of arboreal landscapes."

He leaned back, as if to pull himself away from the innocent pleasure to the business at hand.

"My own fondness for these wonderful creatures aside, they possess three equally wonderful and eminently useful characteristics which we can, gently and with gratitude, exploit."

Braunhut was an expert in paleozoology. Perhaps these sea monkeys or kappa were ancient species still among us, like crocodiles, komodo dragons, or coelacanths. . . .

"Our sea monkey friends are creatures of warmth," Chopek said, "having prospered in this volcanic region for many millennia. Yet they are capable of diving to great depths. It is still a mystery how they breathe. We know that they can ingest oxygen through their lungs and their gills. Their soft bodies seem to be indifferent to the pressures of great depths and find that no impediment. They are also, as I've said, shockingly intelligent. They are trainable, or perhaps more accurately, they are educatable. They can be taught. They can even be motivated. You've seen seals that stand on overturned barrels and clap for a herring. You've seen dolphins that can jump through hoops or monkeys that can insert square blocks into square holes, while avoiding round ones, to secure a peanut or a grape. Those levels of mastery are nothing to the kappa. The kappa, our little sea monkey, can perform complicated tasks. They can be given objectives and solve problems. I will show you soon enough. Moreover, they have a dexterity with their four fingers, even minus a thumb, that rivals a human's. And while they appear slack of muscle and loose in flesh, almost like a jellyfish, it would be a mistake to confuse that with a lack of strength. Their litheness is python-like."

The sea monkey slithered playfully under Chopek's hand.

"But most importantly of all, for our species anyway, and for the future of our civilization, the kappa has a nose for oil. With the help of our friend, here, and his fellows, we have made a great discovery. We have developed a means to identify sources of oil far below the ocean surface. The method is indisputable. Its accuracy total. We no longer need any more guessing. How is not for me to say at the moment, but you will learn in good time. It is up to you, as ingenious scientists, engineers, and managers, to figure out another how—how we will industrialize this endeavour and turn untapped potential into the most secure and reliable source of energy the world has ever known. Tomorrow we begin workshops to problem-solve the challenges that remain.

"For now, I bid you good-day."

The screen went blank.

We gathered in the plaza beneath tables shaded with umbrellas. A number of white-clothed natives milled among us, carrying trays, smiling broadly, serving us bowls of ice cream or cocktails that were a light green in concoction, like dazzling emeralds. I took an ice cream but had no desire to taste it.

My colleagues talked loudly and enthusiastically to each other, strangers engaging with strangers, as happens when people emerge into the light after unusual events. I noticed a small, almost miniature, kappa on a pillar, and another on the edge of a table. Once again, their colouration made them practically invisible until you spotted the peculiar liquid movement. One crawled up the armrest of my Russian companion's chair. I could not help but smile as it neared her flesh. As her spoon went from mouth to bowl and back again, the creature reached with one outstretched limb and clung on suddenly, an unexpected passenger. She screeched in terror and flung the spoon from her hand. The kappa fell flailing toward what had undoubtedly been its desired destination all along, her bowl of ice cream.

Those of us who witnessed what had happened laughed quietly. Others who'd been alarmed by her shriek saw the kappa in her bowl and laughed even harder. The Russian princess did not like to be the cause of mockery. Her eyes blazing at the insult, she struck at the ice cream bowl, overturning it, so that the contents splattered. The kappa landed on the table, indifferent to her assault. Sensing insolence, the Russian brought her glass down hard, as though slamming a shoe onto an offending roach. We grimaced. The kappa wriggled violently away minus its tail.

"Beast!" she shouted in English.

But the crowd had gone silent. The only beast they saw was her.

The tail continued to twist on the table, the nerves still firing, the ice cream smearing below it with a tinge of green that must have been blood or offal. Then something miraculous happened. I saw the wriggling of the tail intensify and the guts excrete from the severed end. But the guts had form. A smaller, more translucent lizard crawling out, birthing itself in the mix of guts and ice cream, attached to the much larger tail, which it dragged now, with difficulty, and slithered across the table and off, plopping to the ground, wriggling away.

"Holy shit," the American nearest me said.

"Regeneration," someone muttered.

Another: "I've heard of lizards growing back their tails, but never a tail growing back its lizard."

"Beast," the Russian princess said.

The native waiters distributed another round of drinks.

We dined buffet style, the assorted seafood not so different from the meal I had made for Nurse Amber on the other island. I saw Hilden and Hans mingling among the scientists and engineers. I saw my icy Russian princess and her Sikh prince. I was beginning to recognize faces and to determine disciplines—the petroleum engineers, the geologists, the chemists, the supply chain managers. I heard snippets of discussion and slices of argument. Calculations around the number of barrels currently being consumed globally versus the number produced. Transport costs. The engineering challenges of drilling at great depths. Seasonal weather patterns. The remarkable taste of the local squid. Then a particularly inebriated and overweight Canadian boasted that he was the best geo-imager on the planet, and would get to the bottom of Chopek's charts before the week was through. His companions hushed him and ordered him coffee with a laugh, whereupon the heavy man fell into his chair, wiping the sweat from his reddened forehead. I wondered if he was allergic to whatever alcohol was in the green glasses. An older Brit made a toast right away to save the moment, thanking Chopek Energy for the hospitality and offering best wishes to all in solving a serious global problem. The majority cheered in response, the merriment returned.

In the darkness, as the feasting went on, I found my moment and slipped away.

My goal was to circle the complex and return to the auditorium in order to gain access to Chopek's private offices. I walked casually, as though out for an evening stroll, but then I saw a figure dart across the walk before me and disappear into shadows. I froze. I waited. I scuffed a shoe deliberately, then I crept to the wall and hid within the shadows myself.

A minute went by, then my adversary appeared, a kimono-clad figure stepping out of the shadow. I reached out, grabbed the arm, and pulled the figure in, cupping my hand across the mouth.

Wriggling in my arms, lithe and strong, but not as strong as me, I kept my hand pressed tight to the mouth even as I gave the hair a forceful tug to show I meant business. The wriggling stopped.

"Amber?" I whispered.

The head nodded. I released.

"What are you doing sneaking into shadows?"

"I'm trying to find a way off of this island."

"Why?"

"Because this place scares me. There's something wrong here. I was drugged this afternoon, Gadsen. I woke without clothes on. I have no memory of anything after I drank the water Hilden poured for me. I think he spiked it."

"Why would he do that?"

"Why would any man?"

"Silly thing. I doubt Hilden had anything like that in mind. He must have wanted you out of the way. The more interesting question is why."

"I don't want to find out why, I just want to leave."

"And how will you do that?"

"There's got to be a boat. Like the one we came in on. We could sail."

"We're a thousand miles from Tahiti. Fifteen hundred from Borneo."

"Have you got a better idea?"

"I do, as a matter of fact. It starts with finding out what's really going on here."

I assumed that my confidence would calm her but instead she gasped. I wondered why for a fraction of a second, and then I sensed the presence of others behind me.

"Dr. Braunhut," a male voice said. "It's a pleasure to meet you."

I did not turn, but remained staring into Nurse Amber's eyes, waiting for any indication or clue as to how I should react.

"Svetlana," the voice continued. "Always good to see you in the field."

Without relinquishing my gaze, Nurse Amber nodded in acknowledgement.

"It is, as you say, a pleasure, Blackburn," she answered, in a distinctly Slavic accent.

I had expected officers of Chopek Energy, but they were my scientific colleagues. Three men. The first was a tow-haired Scandinavian I'd noticed after dinner when the espressos had been distributed. He'd distinguished himself during the social by his sullen quiet and lack of appetite. Now, instead of an espresso cup, he held a snub-nosed .38, which he pointed low at my belly. A shorter Chinese Malay or Indonesian stood beside him, inscrutably expressionless, but in the way his hands dangled I could tell that he had the ability to use them with deadly capacity. Behind them both, the overweight Canadian who had proclaimed himself the greatest geo-imager on the planet. No longer garrulous, his eyes were piercing.

"Are we going to stand here and socialize, Blackburn, or do you have something particular in mind?" Nurse Amber asked, her accent still disconcerting to me. Nothing physically had changed in her appearance, and yet her cheekbones seemed sharper, her eyes ever so slightly Asiatic.

The Canadian, who must have been Blackburn, nodded.

"My hut," he said. "We'll talk there."

The Scandinavian gestured with the gun for us to walk ahead. I noticed that he took more care with Nurse Amber than he did with me.

It was a room like my own. The Scandinavian lowered the gun as soon as we entered. The Chinese moved chairs together. Blackburn gestured for us to sit.

"Are you sure it's not bugged?" Nurse Amber asked.

"Of course I'm sure. Foo Wai is the best in the business."

"Issa Abromovic is the best in the business, but no matter."

"He was. Before that unfortunate incident."

"He will recover."

"Are you certain? It seems unlikely he will be the same man."

"You underestimate."

"Please," the Scandinavian said. "There are more important things to discuss."

"You are right, Gottfried. Let's get down to business. I am impressed, Svetlana. An ingenious way to gain access to the island. Posing as Dr. Braunhut's nurse."

"We determined that Braunhut was the key. What better way to stay close to him?"

"And why do you think Braunhut is so important?"

"Logic, Blackburn. Among all of the petroleum engineers and geologists, only one paleozoologist."

Blackburn smiled. "Of course, we saw that, too. But we did not have your assets. Have you told him?"

"He knows nothing," Nurse Amber said.

"Then how did you know he would cooperate?"

"I have never had any difficulty making a man cooperate."

Blackburn laughed. "That's true. We still tell the

story about the foreign minister's personal aide."

"He does not care much for Vladivostok."

"I'm sure it lost its appeal once he knew you would not be joining him."

"I am a Moscow girl."

"Well, Dr. Braunhut," Blackburn turned to me. "You are very much in the dark. You are confused and probably frightened."

"He does not look frightened," Gottfried said.

"Or confused," Foo Wai added.

"No," Blackburn said. "He is a cool customer, I suppose. In any event, we are here to enlist you in our common cause."

"And what cause is that?" I asked.

"To prevent Dr. Petr Chopek from accomplishing his plan."

"His plan?"

"World energy domination."

I looked about the room at my four inquisitors. A Norwegian. An Indonesian. A Canadian. A Russian. I gave Nurse Amber an especially long look, as though trying to come to terms with her betrayal. She had not revealed my true identity. Why? I decided to play along.

"I see," I said. "You represent non-OPEC oil-producing nations. Why are you threatened by Chopek's plan? Is it because he would increase global supply and render your own resources less valuable?"

"When we learned that he had moved his operations to this island, four years ago, courtesy of our colleague Foo Wai, we assumed that he was continuing his efforts to produce synthetic oil."

"Of course," I said. "Chopek Energy has always been a chemical leader."

"We did not perceive this as a threat of any magnitude since the cost of manufacturing synthetic fuel, and the issues with quality, make for a poor industrial product with little scalability. Our own switch grass and ethanol production capacities are sufficiently advanced to withhold such a challenge."

"But now you believe he actually has the capacity to tap vast reserves of undersea oil."

"Vast, vast reserves," Blackburn said. "What we don't understand is how he is going to, as he put it earlier, eliminate the guess work. We need you to explain what he has in mind with the lizard."

I looked again to Nurse Amber. She appeared unmoved by any plea or concern she might have seen in my eyes. She would have made a world-class chess player. And yet, I believed, at some level, she wanted me to continue with the deception. At any rate, it seemed far more interesting to do so.

"Of course," I began, "I've never studied a species of kappa, or the *sphenomorphus* skink, first hand. I have only studied the fossil record. To see one amble about on the desk, or hop into our boat, was to me what it would be like for you to see a Tyrannosaurus Rex in a zoo. An unthinkably remarkable experience. What I wouldn't give to dissect one. I could advance the field of paleozoology by many decades with one afternoon and a scalpel."

Blackburn lifted his hand to bring an end to my exuberance. "Please, Dr. Braunhut. Focus your attention on the reason why these creatures are so important to Chopek's plans."

I nodded. "Yes, of course. My apologies." I looked about again, and swallowed as though to show that I was in fact nervous and in need of bringing my emotions under control.

"What I mean is that it is impossible for me to know the morphology of the creature without direct examination, but if you will forgive me making wild speculations, I believe I can put forward some baseless but perhaps helpful theories."

"Please," Blackburn said. "Speculate wildly."

"You noticed a slickness to the creature?" I asked.

He nodded.

"And, of course, you noted its remarkable chameleon-like properties?"

"It's what?" Gottfried asked.

"The way it mimicked its immediate surroundings. Its ability to blend its own colouration to match any background."

"Ah, yes, its camouflage."

"Its natural camouflage. Well, these are characteristics I could not have imagined from examining fossils, but in combination with certain things we have seen in the fossil record and with comparisons of ancestors that we know remain alive today, I can make some guess as to how and why Dr. Chopek finds the creatures so fascinating and useful."

"Such as?"

"By its slick, almost translucent skin, I can posit the possibility, for example, that this creature is indebted to oil."

"Indebted?"

"That it needs oil. That it probably derives its lubrication from ingested oil. Most oily species extant today produce their own, such as the otter or seal, which excrete oil onto the skin and trap it within hair follicles to insulate the body from cold water and give it slickness for swimming. However, we have long postulated that primitive species may have relied on external sources before they evolved the innate ability. The kappa may prove this theory to be true. Indeed, in the fossil record, we have noticed cavities in the base of the brain that might be indicative of a natural reservoir for storing oil. The sperm and narwhals, for example, collect the oil they produce within a cavity at the top of the skull, and we presume that this aids those massive creatures in their buoyancy and their ability to self-regulate internal pressure when diving rapidly to great depths. Perhaps this kappa, too, is a deep swimmer."

"That would fit with Chopek's claims."

I nodded vigorously as though pleased by the academic progress we were making.

"I suspect that its glandular system serves as a complex collection, filtration, distribution system for oil."

"Dr. Braunhut, we are not zoologists."

"We're not even geologists," Foo Wai added.

"Apologies," I said. "What I mean is that I suspect the kappa can ingest oil, through its skin or perhaps its gills—since it also has lungs, we naturally wonder if the gills do double duty—then circulate that oil to reservoirs in its head, and perhaps in nodes in the armpits and groin, and use that supply for lubrication, camouflage, and pressurized buoyancy."

"Yes, doctor, but to what end? Why does the kappa matter to Chopek?"

I looked surprised, and took a moment before speaking. "Why, because the kappa are natural oil detectors. They seek oil, sniff it out, I suppose, like a bloodhound."

"There is no oil in water, Braunhut. The two don't mix."

"Of course there is, Mr. Blackburn, you should have studied your geology better. There is always oil in water, especially in water that lies above oil deposits. The earth exudes oil above any deposit, it pools in rock or it turns the soil into tar. The same thing happens below the sea, except the molecules of oil mix with the molecules of water. I presume these kappa, swimming about, detect these molecules and take them in through their gills, not unlike how we take in molecules of oxygen through our lungs."

"Remarkable," Blackburn said.

"I don't believe it," Gottfried said.

I shrugged. "What do you expect? I have not even examined a creature. But I was brought here for some reason. The creature itself is key."

"But the depths," Foo Wai said. "Even if the creature can find the oil deposit. How does Chopek mean to drill at such depths? It's not feasible."

"That is why he has assembled the world's greatest engineers," Nurse Amber said. "It is a grand endeavour. An Azarmas Project."

"A what?" Blackburn said.

"Like Manhattan Project but Russian," Gottfried answered.

"You mean the bomb the Soviets were only able to build because of the spy, Klaus Fuchs?" Blackburn said. I noted a touch of bitterness.

"Comrade Klaus only confirmed what we had already discovered," Nurse Amber said.

"I bet," Blackburn said.

"Stop it," Foo Wai said. "We need to plan our next step."

Blackburn nodded and turned back to me. "You're right, Foo. This is too important. All of our interests are aligned in stopping Chopek. Your health, Dr. Braunhut, it has worsened in the past twenty-four hours."

"No, I feel fine," I said.

"No, it has worsened. And you cannot be parted from Nurse Amber, not even for a minute."

"Oh," I said. "I understand. Yes, it has worsened."

"At some point, Dr. Chopek is bound to give you access to the kappa, perhaps to meet with you in person. Can we rely on you, Svetlana?"

Nurse Amber nodded. "I will do what must be done."

"And we will focus on the facilities."

"I don't understand," I said. "You are going to . . . kill him? Damage the complex?"

"Whatever is necessary, Dr. Braunhut, to save the world from the domination of one man."

Blackburn looked to Nurse Amber who nodded once again.

"It is late," Blackburn said. "We will not acknowledge each other tomorrow, except in casual encounters. We have work to do."

They rose. Reluctantly, I stood as well.

Outside in the darkness, Nurse Amber and I walked silently side by side. The night was still warm, but the heat was no longer stifling. The party must have ended because there was no sound but the scrape of our footsteps, the rustle of leaves in the soft breeze, the distant rush of waves. The stars above were ferociously brilliant and plentiful. I had never seen such stars.

"You did not tell them the truth about me," I said.

When Nurse Amber spoke, it was in her American accent again. Midwestern, I thought. Michigan or perhaps Minnesota.

"You did very well," she said, and I saw a smile. "How did you manage to create such a convincing explanation? Have you been studying paleozoology in your spare time?"

"I'm a dime store novelist, remember? I can write 40,000-word adventure stories in a week."

"You must type incredibly well."

We stopped outside her door.

"Two fingers," I said. "But I am very good with both of them."

"Aren't you coming in?" she asked. "Remember, your condition has worsened. I am not to leave your side."

"Is this how you plan to assure my cooperation?"

She pulled the lapel of my kimono. "I have seen

you do many impressive things over the past few days, Dr. Braunhut. I am very curious about your typing ability."

5

The next three days, I attended lectures and seminars. I gave the appearance of being interested but easily tired. Nurse Amber never left my side. She fed me bits of volcanic clay to give me a clammy pallor and a persistent nausea. Fortunately, the effect wore off before bedtime each night.

The lectures and seminars were fascinating at the outset, but quickly descended into nuance and detail that left any but a dedicated geologist, engineer, or chemist floundering and lost. I sensed in Nurse Amber's tightly held smile a growing impatience. She was clearly a person of action, even in her discretion. Whenever I looked at her and considered who she really was—not an amiable, capable nurse, but a Soviet spy—I remembered my shock when she had fired two rounds into the chest of the thug at the airstrip. Intentional, of course. An execution. The tidying up of loose ends. Would there come a time when I might be considered another stray thread? I had no doubt she would capable of dispatching me just as coldly. Perhaps she would look shocked afterwards, horrified by whatever accident she had unintentionally caused.

Our routine was full but not demanding. Breakfast each morning. A first lecture or seminar at ten. After lunch, there was a recreation hour during which many of the guests took to swimming in the lagoon. They stayed near the shore, but frolicked pleasantly in the water, and they were joined each time by a school of immature kappa. The creatures seemed drawn to the boisterous play and participated to some degree. At first, it was alarming to have such slick and difficult-to-see lizards swimming in and about the throng, and several of the women shrieked and escaped from the water. But the kappa won them over. Swimming on their backs like otters. Propelling themselves to impressive heights into the air like salmon. Nudging humans playfully like seals when a bump was least expected. To my eye, they appeared exceptionally intelligent in their behaviour and mimicked the actions of the swimmers. When confronted directly with a smile or a splash, they disappeared instantly, as though frightened, but then re-emerged above the surface holding some treasure outstretched in one of their four-fingered paws: a piece of coral, a particularly large oyster, or the rusted metal of a harpoon end. Of course, I could not enter the water, being ill, and Nurse Amber lay demurely at my side on the beach towel below the parasol, though I sensed that many of the men and a few of the women could not help but stare when she doffed her kimono and revealed her bikini. A shadow came over me and I looked up to see the Canadian Blackburn standing near my shoulder, hands on his hips as though scanning the horizon. He wore a Speedo bathing suit, almost hidden by an enormous hirsute gut which hung over it like a billowing snow drift. I looked back to the water just as quickly, careful to be nonchalant about his proximity.

"Any progress?" Nurse Amber asked without opening her eyes. I could not imagine how she had noticed him.

"Foo Wai is gone," Blackburn answered, without looking down.

"Escaped?" I said, as though it would be my deepest desire.

"I suspect he has found a way into the industrial laboratories below the complex. He will remain hidden until his absence is noticed or his skills are called upon. He has a remarkable ability to go undetected."

"That will be useful," Nurse Amber said.

Blackburn ambled to the edge of the water, waded in up to his knees, then dove, like a ship plowing through surf. The kappa flittered away, then made a joke of the disruption, smacking the water and sending splashes into the air. Blackburn did not look amused as he floated on his back and watched, though the rest of us smiled or laughed.

The afternoon seminar was followed by ice cream—which had become our traditional break. Then a siesta, dinner, and an entertaining lecture on Captain Cook's first voyage to nearby Tahiti on the appropriately named Endeavour, to observe the famed Transit of Venus. After, there were drinks and conversation for those inclined. I made sure to protest my tiredness early each night.

The next afternoon, at the beach, I noticed an old man standing at the rocks. He was not dressed in a kimono or a bathing suit, but a pair of shortened pants, bare feet, and a long pirate's shirt.

"Chopek?" I whispered to Nurse Amber.

She glanced over and closed her eyes again. "I don't think so," she said. "Chopek was stockier than that, though their ages look to be about the same."

I was amazed and impressed that she could take in so much so quickly at such a distance.

"Whoever it is, I haven't seen him before," I said. "Doesn't that seem odd to you?"

"Perhaps," she answered.

"I feel the urge to look for shells. Would you join me?"

"Of course," she said.

She helped me stand. I actually needed the help because of the clay-induced nausea. We walked to the shore, and to the edge where the waves left smooth sand with its detritus of broken shells. We swept our feet along that mark, turning up shells, occasionally leaning over to pick one up, either tossing it away or holding it in a cupped hand. No one paid us any attention and we made our way to the far end of the beach where the rocks began.

When we were within forty feet I saw clearly that Nurse Amber was right. This man was not Chopek. He was gaunt and older, and as his weathered face became easier to see, any resemblance was destroyed. He stared out at the lagoon and the island across from it, the one we had come from. There was something forlorn in his expression and

I was reluctant to intrude. Still, I wanted to know who he was.

"Ahoy," I called playfully.

He glanced in our direction, then looked back across the lagoon. I feared that he would leave his post before I reached his side. However, Nurse Amber, perhaps deliberately, had loosened her kimono as we neared and it flowed from her shoulders now, revealing her impressive form. This seemed to stay him.

"I'm Dr. Braunhut," I said, "of the delegation, and this is Nurse Amber."

I held out my hand. He did not reach for it, merely stared as though pained by something, and then I realized who I must be standing before. The old captain. Hans Troch's father.

"Captain Troch," I said, "it is an honour to meet you."

And with this he nodded and finally shook my hand with a firm grip. Nurse Amber stood at my side and beamed.

"A sea captain!" she said.

Troch only grunted.

"I gather you discovered this island," I said.

"Before the war," he answered with a thick Dutch accent. "Almost forty years ago now."

"And the kappa?" I asked.

"Discovered those damn lizards, too."

"I think they're so cute!" Nurse Amber said.

Troch grimaced.

"How come they are found only here?" I asked. It was the thing I wanted to know.

Troch muttered an answer but his accent made his words indistinct.

"They're locked in the lagoon," he said.

"What?" I asked.

"They like the lagoon," he repeated.

"Good afternoon, Captain Troch. How wonderful to see you on this side of the island."

Hilden stood behind us. I had not heard him approach.

Troch, if it was possible, became even more sullen and taciturn, not acknowledging Hilden's presence.

"Hilden," I said in greeting.

"Dr. Braunhut, you are feeling well enough for a walk, I see," he said.

"I try to get the blood flowing," I answered.

"With supervision, I hope," Hilden said.

"Of course."

"Speaking of your minder," Hilden continued, "I was wondering if we could borrow her this afternoon while you prepare for your lecture tomorrow."

"My lecture?" I asked.

"Borrow?" Nurse Amber asked.

"Yes, Nurse Amber. We were wondering if you could lead a discussion on nutrition and exercise. Would that be safely within your skill set?"

"Why, I taught a class on nutrition and exercise at Saffron Hills!"

"So we thought. We have about twenty guests signed up. Would you be able to join them in the plaza at three?"

"I'd love to!"

"Then perhaps if you returned now to your room

you would have just enough time to change and prepare."

Nurse Amber looked to me.

"I'll be fine," I said. "Please don't worry about me."

"I will look after him, Nurse Amber," Hilden said.

She turned and left us. We watched her walking away, bare feet digging deep into the sand.

"I hope you've enjoyed your recreation, Dr. Braunhut," Hilden said. "The party is over."

"And what do you mean by that, Hilden?" I asked as we walked back along the beach.

"Only that we're putting you to work tomorrow to give a lecture on the Paleolithic record of salamanders. There is great interest in your research."

"It's unfortunate I won't be able to give the lecture," I said, as I bent over to pick up my towel.

I could feel Hilden tense beside me. He had seemed so confident a moment before.

"Why is that, Dr. Braunhut?" he asked coldly.

I stood and stared at him.

"Because I will not lecture until I've spoken with Dr. Chopek."

I waited. Hilden did not react, but he did not dismiss my threat.

"Dr. Chopek is a busy man, Dr. Braunhut. I've told you before he has little interest in socializing. He has this entire operation to manage. You are only required to give one lecture."

"We both know that Dr. Chopek has no need for the world's great geologists and petrochemical engineers, Hilden. It's me he wants. The only thing I need in return is to talk to him, in person."

Hilden nodded, a grave and unpleasant resolve in the grim tightness of his mouth.

"Alright, doctor. You win. Meet me in the symposium in an hour."

He bowed and left me. Alone, I looked back on the beach and the water abandoned now by the swimmers. I stared across at our island, which Captain Troch had been looking at so recently. I realized suddenly that it was possibly the most beautiful view I'd ever enjoyed in my life. Then a dark spot appeared before me in the water, the sleek head of a kappa, its eyes barely visible above the water line. *They're locked in the lagoon*, I thought, remembering Troch's mutterings. We maintained each other's gaze until the kappa slipped below the surface again, and disappeared.

6

I had showered and put on my best kimono and the padded slippers. When I entered the symposium, I was struck by the way the light within had altered from my previous visit. Then, the sun had been belting the roof above, yet only a filtered refraction had managed passage through the thin gill-like skin of the ceiling. Now, the light was cooler but of a deeper texture with a faintly green colouration. I felt as though I were spending a timeless moment within a cresting wave.

Though I was the only one in the audience, Hilden appeared on the stage. An hour earlier he had seemed tense and impatient; he was smiling now, once again the welcoming representative of Chopek Energy. I was disappointed to see this recovery of confidence, and feared that I'd been tricked. Did my demand to meet Chopek mean that I would only see him on the giant film screen, as we had before? But no, Hilden was waving me toward him.

"Please, Dr. Braunhut, this way."

Because of the strangely effective acoustics, Hilden barely needed to raise his voice. I heard him as though he were standing a few feet before me, not half an auditorium away.

I walked the long aisle then climbed a flight of stairs onto the stage. Glancing back at the auditorium I was astonished to see that its shape, hidden to me before, resembled very clearly the broad snout of a kappa. The gill slits, the two oval windows above the doors. It was as if I were within the primitive head.

"Yes," Hilden remarked, as though he knew exactly what I had discovered. "Dr. Chopek is waiting."

We crossed the broad stage, parted the curtain, and came to a door made of metal. It was like a hatch within a submarine, a round wheel bolted to the front below a small bubble window.

I could not hide my surprise.

"Completely sealed," Hilden said. "Dr. Chopek has preserved his health and vigour, not to mention the purity of his experiments, by carefully controlling his environment."

Hilden turned the wheel. Inadvertently, I held my breath. But when the hatch opened, I released and breathed again.

The tunnel before us was ten or twelve feet high and at least that much across. It was pleasantly lit from slits along the floor with a source I could not identify. Its surfaces were smooth and polished yet retained the organic shape of the tunnel Nurse Amber and I had discovered on the other island.

"This rock," I said to Hilden. "It isn't normal sediment, is it?"

"You're right. Perhaps our geological friends are rubbing off on you, Dr. Braunhut. It's volcanic, of course," Hilden answered. "The tunnels themselves were created through volcanic eruptions when surges of lava travelled through the spongy porous stone, eating away at whatever was not hard, much like termites eat away at the weaknesses in wood and leave meandering trails. Beautiful, isn't it?"

I nodded as though impressed, but Hilden's explanation confirmed something—he was either ignorant of the tunnels' true nature or he was lying.

"We've reached the first cavern," Hilden announced.

The cavern was more raw and natural, less rounded and polished, with an uneven ceiling and corners rich with stalagmites and stalactites. One wall, however, was completely sheer and covered in glass. Behind the glass was an aquarium, large kappa within, darting like otters or seals in a zoo. I counted six or eight in total, though it was difficult to tell as they appeared and disappeared. I walked closer.

"Over a hundred million years old, and they still play like puppies," Hilden said.

It was then that I saw the human corpse within the tank, some twelve or fifteen feet back, partially hidden by a flowery burst of coral. It floated gently in suspension like an astronaut in space. As I watched, the rapid propulsion of the kappa diving and scooting about caused it to shift or bob ever so slightly in the currents. I suppressed my shock and stared. The body turned, a slow-motion twirl, and I saw more. The black hair was short but lifted from the skull as though from electrocution. The hands were outstretched, trying to stabilize an endless plummet. The throat had been ripped jaggedly, the eyes and nose . . . must have been eaten. The dark hair, those hands . . . I recognized the man despite the horrific mauling. It was Foo Wai.

"One of your guests?" I asked Hilden.

Hilden seemed content to take in my shock without turning my way.

"Unfortunately," he began, "this particular delegate was not a pipeline expert after all, but a terrorist. We wanted to have him arrested and returned to his home government but in trying to flee, he slipped into the water. The kappa played with him for hours until he became exhausted and drowned. Then they ate him."

"I assumed kappa ate plankton, krill, shellfish," I said. "Not people."

"You assumed they were not predators?" Hilden said. "Incorrect, Dr. Braunhut. But, I must admit, these kappa are special."

"Special?" I asked.

"Think of them as drones or worker bees or soldier ants. Dr. Chopek refers to them as specimen B. Specimen A is the primitive, smaller variety you have seen in the lagoon, that friendly, delightful, eager-to-please creature. The B-monkey has a bit more . . . determination."

"I see," I said. "Bred for selected traits. Size, temperament, intelligence . . . determination."

"You could say that," Hilden answered. His

amusement at my answer made me feel that I was, in some very important way, off the mark.

We continued our stroll. Although we did not dally, Hilden seemed in no hurry. I suspect he had a specific time of arrival in mind. The passage widened into another cavern, except that this one was not smooth and rounded like the previous but honeycombed with tubular rock formations, as though ventricles to a heart had been severed and left dangling. In some of the odd tubular protuberances, there were white recessed lights, casting the room in a multitude of spotlight glows. In others, elongated glass ends extruded like bubbles of mucus. These appeared to be filled with a viscous green liquid, lit from within. Peering intently, I could see the faint drifting form of something embryonic floating inside each one.

"You rely on artificial breeding?" I asked.

"It's faster," Hilden said. "In nature, the kappa lay several million eggs in a jelly-like mass, which are fertilized by a random male, producing a thousand or so offspring, of which, after natural predators have had their way, approximately three to four immature kappa survive. Dr. Chopek does not like those odds. He has accelerated the life cycle and improved the hardiness of the species by focusing on individual embryos and giving them the nutrition, care, and protection they need."

"And what is their life span?" I asked.

"Forty to fifty years, I'm told."

"Chopek's been studying kappa that long?" I asked, feigning astonishment.

"I think you should ask Dr. Chopek himself," Hilden said.

We had come to another metal hatch sealing the tunnel.

Hilden unscrewed the hatch and swung it open, then gestured for me to enter. Before me was a stainless steel room, square in proportion, drilled with holes, like a cheese grater. At the far side another hatch.

"I will not be accompanying you any farther," Hilden said. "Dr. Chopek is not keen to expose himself to too many people at once."

I hesitated. It would serve my own purposes to meet Dr. Chopek alone. However, it seemed just as likely that I was being set up. Yet, what choice did I have?

"Thank you," I said, and stepped into the room.

Hilden closed the hatch behind me, spinning the wheel to lock it. I stepped forward across the strange grated surface and grasped the wheel on the other hatch. It did not budge. I tried more forcefully.

A hissing sound. A vapour-like mist suffused the room from every surface at once.

I expected the worst, and covered my mouth with a fold of kimono. I could feel the mist on my skin, and sensed it had an activated property—a sensation of burning cold not unlike a dab of tiger balm on the skin. The mist did not attack my eyes. When I could no longer hold my breath, I found it stimulating to the throat and lungs. Like a cool inhalation of peppermint.

Within a minute, the hissing stopped and the mist retreated as though vacuumed away. A distinct clicking sound on the hatch led me to believe that a lock had been released. I grasped the wheel and twisted again—this time it gave way, and the door itself popped out. I stepped into a larger room.

Hans Troch, the captain's son, stood before me. He had changed his clothes and his hair looked flatter. He smiled warmly and welcomed me with enthusiasm to Dr. Chopek's private quarters. The room before me was spare and austere, a touch sterile. The floor and walls were covered in a kind of pale blue tile I had seen in certain mosques in Indonesia. There was a smell of clean water in the air, and I saw several standing pools, constructed out of a darker lapis lazuli tile. I ignored Hans and walked over to the first pool to look within. I expected for some reason to see diminutive kappa inside, perhaps in some pollywog-like state, but there was only water, rippling and clear.

Hans remained in place, watching me without suspicion or haste. I took in the rest of the room. A long banquet table. Another living room area where there were a few comfortable chairs and a low coffee table. There was a silver tea set on the table, a plate of English powder biscuits alongside. I looked up at the loft with a desk and the broad window overlooking a particularly verdant and pleasant forest outside—was this where Chopek had filmed his presentation to the delegates?

"I don't see Dr. Chopek, Hans," I said calmly. "Perhaps you could explain."

Hans did not seem concerned in the slightest.

"Oh, he'll be here soon enough. Be patient."

A moment later, an elevator door in the far corner of the room slid open. Nurse Amber walked in. She was dressed in a spectacular kimono, royal blue in colour, printed with a floral burst of pink and yellow flowers budding from the branches of a gold brocade tree. She was not smiling. She appeared to be walking stiffly. Dr. Petr Chopek followed her into the room.

He walked slowly also. He was smaller than he had seemed in his auditorium projection, more advanced in age. He was dressed as I have seen some Indonesian royalty dress, in a long batik skirt, which hung to the floor, bare feet, and a grey Nehru jacket that seemed two sizes too big for him and hung loose at that peculiar priest-like collar. His hair was white and thin. His eyes, even from a distance, dazzled blue. He smiled but there was something pained about the way the lines in his face creased together. Nurse Amber reached Hans and me. At about ten feet away, Chopek stopped. He did not extend a hand, and did not seem to move any muscles that he did not have to move. In person, I was struck by the peculiar appearance of his skin, somehow waxy, gleaming, and chapped all at once, eczemic and yet supple.

"What a pleasure," Chopek said, though he did not look as though he were experiencing pleasure when he spoke. "We finally meet."

"His name is Gadsen Wells," Nurse Amber said suddenly, her accent distinctly Slavic once more.

"He knows nothing. He is an amateur adventurist with an over-active imagination. The real Braunhut is dead."

"Oh, I know about the poor unfortunate Braunhut," Chopek said, a smile finally forming with a very deliberate broadening of his lips. "After all, we found his body trapped in the wreckage of your plane. But Braunhut's doppelganger is also welcome."

"He is only a dime store novelist," Nurse Amber said. "Not a scientist, not even a spy."

"You really do not know!" A laugh of delight from Chopek, a burst of surprise that seemed to cause him pain. "Gadsen Wells, may I introduce you to our fair representative of Soviet intelligence?"

I nodded. "Go ahead."

"Svetlana, meet John Conover Junior, the son of my greatest rival, the American inventor, businessman, and adventurer, Mr. Howard Robard Hughes."

"The bastard son," I corrected.

Dr. Chopek bowed in acquiescence. Svetlana said nothing, but it was plain that her astonishment and confusion were sincere.

Chopek invited us to sit at the banquet table for a meal. He took the head of the table, and allowed me to sit at the other end while Svetlana and Hans sat across from each other in the middle. It was awkward to be so spread apart, but Chopek seemed more comfortable with physical distance.

"Would you mind, Hans?" Chopek said.

Hans stood and began to remove the silver tops from the trays on the table, naming each dish as he revealed it. The food was familiar to us by now, harvested from the sea, various fish, shellfish, and cephalopods, accompanied by sea weed, diced jelly fish, scoops of urchin.

"Please excuse the lack of formality," Chopek said, "but I ask you to kindly serve yourself as much or as little as you would like. I assure you that this is the most nutritious and among the most delicious food on the planet."

I glanced cautiously at Svetlana. It was worrisome to see her so contained and tepid. With her sluggish, awkward motions I wondered if she had been drugged or worse . . . perhaps beaten so badly that she was suffering internal injuries.

In spite of everything, I was hungry and served myself generous portions, particularly the sea urchin which I heaped like oddly coloured yoghurt on a side plate. Hans, too, seemed to enjoy the feast. Only Chopek did not indulge. Instead of a plate he had a single silver glass, and beside it a crystal pitcher. It looked to be filled with lemonade.

"You do not join us in eating, Dr. Chopek?" I asked.

Hans looked displeased by my directness, but Chopek did not seem perturbed.

"I forego most meals in place of a citrus refreshment with an acidic content of precisely three percent."

I nodded. "My father, I'm told, does the same."

"Is his pain unbearable?" Chopek asked.

"At times," I answered. "Like you, he has isolated himself from the world because of his caution with germs. He finds wearing clothes difficult. Cutting his hair and nails, even washing, can be nightmarish. This is what I am told."

"Then, like me, he is still seeking. Or perhaps you are seeking for him."

Svetlana put her fork down suddenly. "I do not believe you are the son of that millionaire," she said to me.

Chopek laughed again. "To call Howard Hughes a millionaire is very amusing. You are in the company of the only living heir to one of the largest fortunes in the world."

I tried to mollify Svetlana's communist outrage.

"I receive a small annual stipend, nothing more, and I like to think that I make my own way, without help or hindrance from my biological father. I have no expectation of inheritance. Howard Hughes's interests are in advancing science. He is particularly judicious with his money when it comes to relations."

Chopek laughed. "Did you know that your grandfather and my father were also rivals, Conover?"

"I assumed that their paths had crossed," I answered. "But I did not know there was any antagonism between them."

"It started there, I assure you. H. R. Hughes, your grandfather, was present at the creation, you could say."

"The creation of what?" Svetlana asked.

"The creation of the modern oil industry," Chopek

answered. "H. R. worked at Spindletop, with all of the other titans, but whereas everyone else saw great gushing oil, H. R. grasped the thing that was more valuable than oil. Within a year, he had patented the two-cone rotary drill bit which was used for the drilling. The design, of course, was stolen from my father, the chief engineer at Spindletop who had failed to recognize the commercial value of his own work. No matter. It was a good lesson, which I have not forgotten."

"As a businessman, you are known for surrounding your assets thoroughly," I observed. "Typical of a paranoid megalomaniac."

Hans, who had been lifting his spoon to his mouth, stopped at my impudence. Chopek's smile did not diminish but did seem colder, as though I had struck a nerve. He summoned patience before answering.

"You resemble your impractical great uncle, the novelist, more than your father or grandfather," Chopek answered. "Has anyone told you that?"

"I have seen the photographs," I said.

"He drank heavily, of course. Perhaps it was frustration. Perhaps a deeper psychological malaise. No wonder you wasted so much of your life writing. Forgive me. It is not meant as a criticism. Only, I have never understood the reason for conjuring fantasy when mastering the world itself is the greatest possible act of creation."

"Perhaps it is because I have seen what men who attempt to master the world do to those around them."

Chopek leaned forward in his chair, the first indication of engagement I had noticed.

“The price, on an individual scale, to lesser beings, can be high, I admit,” he began. “But for humanity, the benefits of world mastery are extraordinary, don’t you agree? What was it Mao said in assessing the impact of Napoleon three hundred years later? Too soon to tell.”

“Then what is your grand vision, Dr. Chopek?” I asked. “You have made a great fortune selling oil. You have exiled yourself to a paradise in the South Pacific. What plans do you have for humanity’s benefit?”

“The evidence is all around you, Conover. Why don’t you guess?”

“Guess?” I said. I put my fork down. “Like my father, you share a fascination with the undersea world.”

“A fascination that he introduced me to.”

“A polite way to say that you spied on him.”

“And he spies on me in return.”

“I am not a spy.”

Chopek shrugged, as if bemused. I slipped the spoon into the fold of my kimono.

“Like my father, I suspect you are engaged in genetic research, and on the intermingling of distinct species.”

“We share a fascination with the origins of life. I like to think that my interests are more practical, however.”

“Yes,” I said. “You are interested in energy in a way that my father never was.”

"Your father is a romantic, at heart. I am inclined toward more fundamental problems."

"And you think the kappa, or your genetically modified subspecies, are key to the fundamental problem of energy."

"In a way that you cannot imagine."

"You use them."

"We use each other. Think of my relationship to the kappa as a kind of merger."

"The kappa are organized."

Chopek nodded, and indicated that I should continue.

"The kappa are intelligent."

"They are a civilization," Chopek corrected.

"The kappa are in competition with us," I said.

"We have interests in similar resources, it's true."

"The kappa are a threat to humanity," I suggested.

"Insofar as humanity is a threat to the planet."

"The kappa will attack us."

"Only to the extent that creation requires destruction, and domination must be accompanied by subjugation."

"Oil. They sniff it out for you. They are your guess removers."

Chopek laughed. "I overheard your wonderful hypothesis when you were talking to your colleagues. We have cameras and microphones everywhere, of course. But you were wrong, I'm afraid, however ingenious your powers of storytelling."

"How was I wrong?"

Lifting my hand to push back my hair, I worked the spoon down my forearm. It fell into the space by my stomach and came to rest on my lap inside the kimono.

"In every way," Chopek said, "except that the kappa are involved."

"If they do not find oil for you, how do they help you exploit it?"

"Have you observed any use of oil on this island? We are not interested in oil. We are beyond petroleum."

I was stopped short by the sudden realization. So obvious all along. And yet, so unthinkable.

"Geothermal," I said.

Chopek's smile was his widest yet. I hoped that it pained him.

I thought of the strange tunnels. The volcanic rock. The legends that linked salamanders to fire.

"But," I began, "if you are truly not interested in petroleum . . . why have you gathered the world's greatest scientists, engineers, and geologists? What need do you have of them?"

"Isn't it obvious?" Chopek offered. "You disappoint me."

And then I understood.

"You are trying to cripple your energy competitors, even as you develop a radical new source of energy."

"I have no competitors anymore, Conover," Chopek said. "But I do wish to increase the helplessness of those who would thwart me. If the nations do not bow, I will destroy the great oil fields of the surface world from within, siphoning them out. At the end of my life there is only one thing I still need to buy."

"A little time," I said.

Chopek rose from his chair. Hans rose instantly, like a shadow.

"Would you like to see my kappa in their element?"

I slipped the spoon into my fist and rose.

Chopek walked slowly to the elevator. Silently, Svetlana followed him, moving tentatively, like one who was also in pain. Hans gestured me forward. There was a shininess to his skin, a waxy, lubricated sheen. I caught up to Svetlana and pressed closer as we entered the elevator. During that moment of tightness I pushed the spoon into her hand.

The elevator was large enough to park a Cadillac in. Chopek stood at some distance from us without touching the wall. He looked weary. The doors closed. The elevator began to move. There was barely any sound to indicate progress, but I sensed that we were descending at great speed.

That speed became obvious when the elevator suddenly stopped. We lurched and staggered, and Nurse Amber's knees folded and she fell into me. A red light on the wall began to blink in some kind of warning. Hans reached for it, a panel fell open, and inside was a black telephone receiver. He brought it to his ear and listened for ten seconds, then placed the receiver back on its cradle and closed the panel.

"It would seem that we are under attack," Hans said. "Should we return to the surface?"

"Nonsense," Chopek said. "It is not unexpected. Our plans will hold."

I shared a glance with Nurse Amber. Did she

know of this attack? I saw in the blankness of her expression that she was as uninformed about it as I was.

"Proceed," Chopek said. At his command, the elevator began to move again.

This time it slowed more gradually. The doors opened. The heat and humidity was such that I felt its thickness immediately. It was as though we had descended to the boiler room of a great ship, or perhaps Hell itself. Chopek gestured for us to precede him. Hans made way, reluctantly, watchfully.

I stepped out.

There was a hissing and bubbling sound coming from everywhere at once, a white noise at high volume that seemed to conspire with the other sensations to obliterate any clarity of thought. We were in an enormous cavern filled with such brilliance and shadow that my eyes could not stand it at first, nor take it all in.

I tried to grasp the meaning.

The darkness was the darkness of shadow, but it was of such inky black purity it seemed no light could ever pierce it. The disorienting brilliance was a crusted white phosphorescence that seemed to cling, like a floral algae or a caked soot, to the ripples of the cave walls and much of the floor. It was the only light, yet like no source I had ever seen before. I had the distinct and sudden fear that I was deep within the Earth and being exposed to secrets not meant to be revealed, that there were mysteries to the composition of the planet, and its shadow landscape, that surface dwellers should never know.

The hissing was steam, but the acrid smell that accompanied the mist, though not poisonous like sulphur, was an irritant to the eyes as well as the mucus membrane of the nose and the soft palette. I could hear Svetlana coughing, and thought of her, in that instant, as Nurse Amber again. I tasted sweat on my own lips. Could the source of the irritant be salt water? The bubbling sound, accompanied by waves of heat, must have been magma. Unlike lava I had seen in movies, it did not give off a red glow but seemed part of the shadow. It was only when I looked closely that I noticed some of the shadow undulating in a slow, distinctive way. The rock of this place, I realized, was not completely solid. Patches of it were semi-liquid in form and practically invisible to the eye, like quicksand. I felt my heart pounding harder at the danger this represented.

"Follow me, please," Chopek said in a raised voice in order to be heard above the dull, ambient groan.

To stray even a few feet from Chopek's path was to invite certain death. I placed my hand on Nurse Amber's shoulder to keep her on track.

And yet I could tell, within moments, that we were actually following a path illuminated by the chalky, brilliant phosphoresce. Discovering the ability to see, to some degree, where we were going, allowed me to relax that part of my brain and concentrate on other matters.

"I am curious, Dr. Chopek," I called out. "Do you really think that geothermal power can replace oil?"

He glanced back over his shoulder and then gestured for me to come up alongside him.

Reluctantly, I left Nurse Amber in Hans's care.

"Of course it can," Chopek answered. "It's completely scalable. You can heat and power an entire city, even operate its transportation system, with a single geothermal plant. The trick is tapping the Earth's core."

I noticed that his face did not seem as pained now. Perhaps the heat and humidity relieved him of the constant agony, much the way that natural hot springs alleviates the symptoms of those with skin and joint ailments. Absurdly, I made a mental note to tell my father, thinking perhaps he would be grateful. As if I ever saw him.

"Then why do you need to subjugate the planet in order to provide it with energy?" I asked. "Wouldn't we all be grateful for your discovery? The capacity of geothermal must be limitless compared to oil."

"It is limitless," Chopek said, "but I doubt your world would be grateful."

My world, I thought. Not Chopek's world, apparently. Not anymore.

"And why is that?" I asked.

"It is one thing to tap geothermal energy at the natural gaps in the planet's tectonic plates. It is quite another thing to tap that energy where there is not a natural gap. Here along the Ring of Fire, we do not need to drill, we only need to position our energy pumps precisely and extract what is otherwise being wasted as magma and steam spilling into the deep waters of the Pacific. But how do you heat and power Chicago, for instance? Or Beijing? Or Moscow? Or Sao Paulo?"

I struggled to come up with an answer. Chopek did not bother to wait.

"You need to create a deep penetrating fissure in the Earth's crust. You need to develop a new kind of energy grid, a system of tectonic fault lines connecting the largest cities on the planet."

I thought of an active volcano in Central Park, a daily earthquake near the Louvre.

"Who would want such a thing? The constant threat of annihilation by the natural forces of the planet would be too much for any society to bear!"

Chopek allowed a smile. "Now you understand why I will be resisted."

I struggled to control my own reeling mind.

"How?" I asked, and only managed to funnel my questions into coherent words with effort. "How do the kappa tap geothermal energy?"

"It is their natural element," Chopek said. "They are drawn to extremes of heat as a place to lay their eggs. Instead of laying eggs, however, I have taught them to conduct feats of engineering. They guide drills, lay pipe, and insert small thermonuclear devices exactly where they are needed to create new tectonic plates."

"I see," I said, defeated by the confidence Chopek exuded.

"You will see," he answered, and I realized we had come to a new cavern.

It was not a natural cave. Even in these depths, where any shape seemed possible, it was clear that the space within had been carefully hewn.

In a sense, it was as if a volcano had been flipped upside down. We stood, at the base, on the surface of the caldera. It was the same rock as the previous room, and dotted with pock marks of convulsing magma, but rounded at the edges, a perfect circle. The walls broadened conically as they rose until they disappeared into darkness at some incalculable distance above. In the centre of the conical space, hanging like a suspended teardrop, was a giant elongated vase of water, wide and open at the top, about fifty feet in height, and perhaps a hundred feet in diameter at its broadest point, narrowing to a delicate three or four foot diameter stem at the base. Inside, was a kappa, larger by a third than any human, and unmistakably female in its naked form with protruding breasts and a smooth pubis. It swam to the edge of the glass when we entered, and pressed against the surface with its peculiar four-fingered hands, then flipped about, as though in excitement or pleasure, before returning to its watchful spot. I saw a smile that was feminine and intelligent, and for that reason, all the more awful to behold.

"My Queen," Chopek said proudly. "The first and primary C-Monkey. Half human. Half kappa. The merger of our species. The mother of a new race to populate the planet."

I gazed at him in horror.

"And her warriors," he continued, and waved his arm to the walls.

I looked to where he indicated. Every twenty feet along that rounded wall there was a tier or band of recessed caves, like a precise series of alcoves. The porousness and symmetry reminded me, once again, of honeycomb. In each alcove there stood a single kappa, hundreds, if not thousands of them in total. Like sentries at attention, utterly still, each with a trident in its left hand as though waiting for Chopek's command. We, under their watchful gaze, stood in some giant panopticon.

"They are statues!"

It was Nurse Amber's voice. She was forgotten behind me. But I saw that she was right. The immobility. Each figure was identical, around six feet in height, muscular, noble-looking, and fixed in position, as though cast from a single bronze mold.

"Not statues," Chopek said. "In stasis. They will be roused when needed."

Chopek approached the glass vase and put his hand onto the surface, a loving gesture. The Queen swam down to be close to him and hovered there, her own fingers pressing next to his. There was an altar-like stand at waist height, an array of switches and dials displayed on it. Chopek ran his finger along the dials as though checking specific readings. Then he looked back.

"My Queen needs a companion to play with. I had hoped, Svetlana, you wouldn't mind going for a swim."

"No!" Nurse Amber cried.

"Hans, seize her."

I turned around but Hans had already grabbed Nurse Amber by the shoulders, and twisted her kimono so that it pinned her arms back. Nurse

Amber, suddenly, with a litheness and agility that had seemed beyond her until that moment, slid from her kimono as though shedding a skin and swung her fist toward Hans's face. The blow knocked him back a step, out of her grasp. In one hand, he still held the shed kimono. His other hand reached for the spoon that was now embedded in his neck.

I expected blood, a fan of arterial spray, but only a dull green ooze seemed to come from the horrifying wound. Still, it seemed as though Hans could not speak, and his neck pulsed and strained like the gills of a fish gasping on dry land. He sank to his knees.

From the hidden fold of his own jacket, Chopek pulled a long-nozzled handgun which he directed toward Nurse Amber. She crouched in anticipation of the shot.

"My patience is finite, Svetlana. Come forward or die where you are."

He flinched, his finger drawing tighter on the trigger.

I threw myself into him. A slam into his body that took him utterly by surprise.

Even so, and in spite of his frail appearance, he was far stronger than I expected. Rocked off balance, he managed to twist toward my direction, the gun levelling again, but this time pointed at me. His heels, however, were at the edge of a pool of magma. He seemed to sense this, but instead of righting himself, took the opportunity to shoot. I heard, rather than saw, the bullet blow by my ear. In the next instant, Chopek's arms began to flail and he gave up all pretense of control. The gun flew from his hand but it did not prevent the inevitable. He stepped backward, inexorably, an innocent step and a horrifically fatal one, into the magma behind.

At first, his face expressed only shock and wonder. In spite of myself, I lunged for him involuntarily, grabbing a hand. He sank slowly into the thick sludge. Suddenly, the hand of rescue became a hand of doom. His grip turned fierce beyond the strength of anything I had ever felt before. He sank deeper, to the waist, and paused, as though some ballast had been achieved. To my horror, I saw the magma dissolving him at that mark, eating through his clothes, his skin, his innards. I must have been still pulling backward, either to free him or to free myself, for suddenly, when the weight of the man was halved, he came flying upward and flopped like a landed fish on the ground before me.

It was an awful sight to behold.

Amazingly, there were no entrails, though he had been bisected neatly. The torso below mid-waist was gone, but the gaping wound had been seared shut by the extreme temperature, cauterized. One hand still gripped mine, the other flung itself wildly about, like a tree branch in a hurricane. All the severed and seared nerve impulses came alive in revolt. He twisted. He writhed violently. He slapped his free hand hysterically against the ground, pounding in futile protest at his thwarted greatness. He was making an odd quacking screech, an utterly inhuman cry, jaw tilting upward, nostrils flaring, eyes bulging, torturous heat still travelling upward along his spinal column and through his remaining entrails. Suddenly, the skin of his forehead split, the terrible heat having worked its way to his face, and he burst like an overcooked sausage, spitting the grease of human fat. . . . The split in his forehead grew wider, dividing his face, destroying the last of his likeness, but instead of bone and the ooze of eyeballs and brains, something gleaming and slick came pouring out as though another creature, slug-like and parasitic, had been encased within his torso. Whatever it was died there on the ground before us like an insect in struggle to be free of its cocoon, stuck half in some pupae state, partially liquid, helpless, unformed.

I turned around. Nurse Amber was behind me, her hands to her face, horrified.

"We must leave!" I said. "We need to find a way out!"

"Not yet," she said.

She turned to the Queen in the glass teardrop.

The smile was gone from the Queen's face, her playfulness also gone. She loomed above us, hovering in the liquid—ominous, powerful, darkly wrathful.

"You bitch," Nurse Amber said.

She had Chopek's gun in her hand. She raised it now. Pointed it at the Queen. I remembered the moment at the airport, a million years ago, when she had fired two slugs into the chest of some other man, now forgotten.

"No!" I yelled.

The bullet struck the glass and splintered an erratic circle that neatly framed the Queen's face.

The Queen looked shocked, momentarily, at this unexpected and impertinent threat, then—when the bullet failed to reach her, repelled or deflected away—her face became angrier still and she raised her arms like a sorceress summoning darkness to her aid.

Without altering her widened stance, without flinching or hesitating, Nurse Amber fired again, the second bullet completing the journey the first bullet had attempted.

I saw the Queen's forehead pocked suddenly by a gaping hole. I saw her body flung a short distance back, even as it was jerked suddenly forward, far more violently and with velocity, pulled headlong toward us. I did not understand why this speed, this tremendous gravitational draw, and felt only the fear of nightmare, the vision of a witch flying in to tear us to pieces. Then I saw the hydrant-like spray of water spewing from the hole in the glass. In the next moment, before I had time even to process the inevitable conclusion, the hole exploded and the contents within rushed out.

The water struck the magma. The explosion of steam lifted me into the air and threw me into the darkness of eternity.

7

When I awoke, I did not know if a minute had passed or a day. I could not see or hear. I touched my eyes, worried now that I had no eyes to see with any longer, or that their usefulness had come to an end. But it was only soot caked to my face, as though I were a miner who had come up from a seam of coal.

I lay in an alcove. I did not know whether I had been flung there or had crawled. Looking out from my shelter, I saw a boiling sea of Hell before me. Perhaps it was for the better that I could not hear, though I could feel the whelp of heat thudding against the cavern walls like the protest of some roused leviathan, angry, all powerful, destructive. It was, I imagined, what it must be like to sit inside the eye of a storm, if that storm was the imminent explosion of a thermonuclear device.

I was alone in this Hell. I did not see any sign of Nurse Amber.

I felt my way around, veering from the heat like an insect without reason, and crawled to the back of the alcove to be as far from it as possible.

The alcove, it turned out, was a tunnel. I followed its trail on my hands and bloody knees.

When I emerged on the surface, I found myself in a thicket of vines and waxy leaves. It was daylight. I was naked, without a shred of cloth to cover me. My hair was a seared and bristly thatch. My hands were swollen with blisters already coming to life, as though I were being attacked virally from within. Around me, still more chaos. I could hear now, though not clearly. Explosions, gunfire, the whistle of incoming mortars.

Keeping to my hands and knees, I crawled under the brush and peered out onto the plaza.

A day before it had been a calm and peaceful square. Now it was a battle zone. I saw kappa, like panthers, flinging themselves through the air and landing on the backs of fleeing scientists, rending throats, tearing off heads. I saw Blackburn and the Scandinavian and a dozen other men dressed in black tracksuits holding Uzis and spraying bullets in controlled bursts into the kappa racing for them. Each kappa that was struck seemed to writhe in green plasma until the torturous twisting produced two or even three more kappa, birthed in wrath. Above, the sky itself seemed to be on fire. It roared orange and red, split and fractured by electric bolts with streaking plume-trailing cast of meteorites flinging themselves in every direction. The island itself was quaking, and I understood in that instant that it was nearing some critical limit of cohesion and about to scatter its mass into smithereens.

The squad of black-clad militia fell back, spraying more bullets even as they lost ground, and were taken down, one by one, by the ceaseless violence of swarming kappa. The civilian scientists, abandoned now, lay at odd angles, draped across tables, fountains. Other bodies, too, all lifeless. As an emptiness suddenly came across the plaza, I found myself running before I had even considered the odds or the purpose. I was running toward the beach and the bay.

When I reached the edge of the water I stood there, helpless, at the nearness of the island across the bay, and the impossible gap between us. The sky roiled even more fiercely than before, as though magma were cascading from above, smoke and meteors like flares and fireworks shooting pell mell. I would swim. I must swim. I had only to swim. I stepped one foot into the water, and was pulled violently back.

"Klootzak!"

Captain Troch gripped my neck.

"Not in the water! This way!"

He pulled me after him. I followed, limping, dragging my leg, but gathering determination as I saw where he was taking us, toward the end of the beach and a rowboat.

We reached it, grabbed a side each, lifted, and hauled it to the water.

"In! In!" Troch shouted at me.

I jumped in the boat, struggling for balance, and grabbed one of the oars. Troch gave us one final shove and followed.

We took an oar each and pulled mightily on it, sliding us away from shore and slowly across the bay.

I kept my eyes fixed on the horror we were leaving behind. It was only when we were halfway across the bay that I saw her standing on the sand.

She was naked. She was scorched like me. But she was standing tall. She flailed her arms at us in signal. She shouted but no sound reached us.

"Troch! Look!" I called.

"It is too late!" he yelled.

"No!" I said, and I struggled with him to turn the boat around. To his credit, and in spite of what we were fleeing, Troch soon gave up his resistance and endeavoured with me to reach her.

She would not wait. She waded into the water. We called out for her to turn back. She swam toward us, strong strokes, like an Olympic swimmer, her torso half above the surface, her arms long, her kicks powerful, her shoulders turning as she tilted her chin, every five strokes, for a breath of air. She had almost reached us when they came.

They slithered under the water like writhing eels. Mercifully, she noticed them just seconds after we did. We stretched out for her with our oars, even though we were still several yards too far away. When she understood what was happening, felt the shock of their teeth and rending claws, she still fought and churned to bring herself closer. Whatever was left of her, still beautiful, still imbued with will, actually reached my oar before life slipped from her fingertips, and she was pulled in a pink froth below the surface of the water, sliding into oblivion.

We had no time to mourn. The kappa were swarming the sides of the boat now, trying to pull the oars from our grasp, trying to climb over the gunwale, trying to jostle and tip us over. We stood and fought like madmen, striking them back, kicking when the oars were stuck, overwhelmed by their numbers, knowing that to pause, even for a breath or a glance about, was to succumb that much quicker to certain doom.

And yet, somehow, we made it to the far shore.

I did not know whether it was the ruckus we created that continued our momentum or whether some great seismic fluctuations in the water below undulated us closer to the sand, but we reached it, and stuck there, nose into the grit. We jumped from the boat and ran for the cave mouth, even as the kappa came up the sand.

Troch lit a dynamite stick as he ran, tossing it over his shoulder. The explosion compressed the world and released it anew, scattering kappa everywhere, clearing the sand for a moment, before more emerged from the writhing bay and slithered low to the ground, tails sweeping behind them, eyes gleaming, teeth bared, chasing us.

Troch left his last stick at the mouth of the cave and we ran as fast as we could down the tunnel. The concussed blast, when it came, flung us faster still and turned us over so that we tumbled headlong in the dust and rocks.

I shook Troch awake and dragged him at first until life came to his legs and he began to limp under his own power again.

"Do you have any more sticks?" I asked as we ran, knowing the kappa would eat through the rock in no time.

"All gone," he said.

It was a pity. Even one more stick would have been enough. It would have been better to emerge from the tunnel and stare at the freedom of the battered shore on the other side of the island for a moment before we blew ourselves up. Much better than waiting for the kappa to come.

"There is nothing for us to do," I said, when we came into the light. But Troch was already pulling my arm.

"We go up!" he said. "Up!"

I did not understand. He meant to climb. I followed him. He was like a billy goat, grasping clefts, clawing upward, navigating natural fissures on the volcanic sheath of the russet-coloured hill. *Would it be better to die up here?* I wondered. It seemed as pointless as anywhere. We rose nevertheless.

I thought we would strive for the peak, but Troch had other ideas. About two thirds of the way to the top, he flattened himself along an edge and began to slide sideways around the curve of the mountain, then disappeared. When I reached the curve myself, I saw a hand stretched out for me and grasped it, then used the leverage to pull my way into a cave.

Inside the cave was an ancient biplane made of balsa wood, lacking even a propeller and a motor.

Troch was already pulling off the burlap sacking. I helped him from the other side, raising dust. Troch pulled the chocks away from the wheels and leaned into the plane until it backed away from the cave entrance by several feet.

"Get in!" he ordered.

I did not want to abandon him, but his intent and

determination were fearsome to behold. I climbed the steps and into the foremost of the two seats. There was a steering stick, and a handwritten letter tacked to the dash.

Below, Troch released his lean against the plane and it began to roll forward. He scrambled up and joined me in the seat behind even as the momentum of the plane and angle of the cave floor brought us at ever-building speed to the mouth and the doom of the plummet below.

We did not plummet, however, not exactly. We tipped, we fell, we caught air, we rose. I pulled back on the stick and the flaps began to do their work, and then, as the island beyond the bay exploded, we propelled like a jet across the ocean and away.

The biplane glided with an unexpected grace, once the turbulence had fallen away. We could manage ten or twenty miles, I guessed, before our slow descent into the Pacific became inevitable. Troch seemed to sense this. At first, he banged the sides of the biplane in victory, and slapped my shoulders and head, and yelled that it worked, that he was an engineering genius. Then he sobered and became quiet, and we heard only the silence of the air around us, and the muffled destruction in the distance behind.

I glanced down at the letter tacked to the dash, and although I could not read the language, I could tell somehow that it was a letter of promise to someone, perhaps to Troch's loved one, a totem of determination to come home, after thirty years of exile.

"I am sorry about your son," I said. I did not know if he could hear me. But Troch answered.

"He has been gone for years," he said.

I hesitated and then wondered.

"Like Chopek?" I asked.

There was no answer. But I could discern affirmation in Troch's silence. What a lonely existence it must have been for him on that accursed island.

"I'm sorry about your lady friend," Troch said.

And I let my own silence serve in answer, too.

"At least I did not die on that island," Troch said, after we had been flying for an hour. "At least those kappa did not make our end."

"We're not dead yet," I said.

"It is okay," Troch said. "I do not mind drowning. As long as the sea is willing to have me."

"Perhaps you should wait until we reach that ship," I said, and pointed to the speck on the horizon.

He did not believe me at first, and then, as we neared and he saw what a strange and monstrous ship it was, he did not understand.

"It is my father's ship," I explained. "The Gomar Explorer."

"But I have never seen such a thing. It is like a city."

"It is unique," I said. "A floating city. An exploration vessel. A drill rig. A scientific research facility. It has been searching for Chopek's island and the kappa for years."

"Your father is on it?" he asked.

I shook my head. “My father, like Chopek, resides in solitude. But he will know we have arrived. I wish I had more to bring him than stories. He would want to study the kappa first hand.”

“We have this,” Troch said, and he thrust his fist over my shoulder and before my eyes. I looked down. The fist opened. Inside Troch held a mound of peculiarly uniform sand granules.

“What is it?” I asked.

“Eggs,” he answered. “They do not live until they are immersed in sea water. Then the kappa sprout. As many as you could want. A whole civilization, if you are not careful.”

“Troch,” I said. I did not know if I meant it in congratulations or in warning.

Troch pulled his hand back and clapped me on the back once more.

“I will die a very rich man,” he said. “Finally.”

We descended toward the liner that waited on the surface of the vast and tranquil sea.

GAMIFICATION

by KEITH HOLLIHAN

CZP

ChiZine Publications

FIRST EDITION

Distributed in Canada by
HarperCollins Canada Ltd.
1995 Markham Road
Scarborough, ON M1B 5M8
Toll Free: 1-800-387-0117
e-mail: hcorder@harpercollins.com

Distributed in the U.S. by
Diamond Book Distributors
1966 Greenspring Drive
Timonium, MD 21093
Phone: 1-410-560-7100 x826
e-mail: books@diamondbookdistributors.com

Library and Archives Canada Cataloguing in Publication

Hollihan, Keith
[Novels. Selections]
Gamification / Keith Hollihan.

A flip book.
Issued in print and electronic formats.
ISBN 978-1-77148-151-9 (pbk.).--ISBN 978-1-77148-152-6 (pdf)

I. Title. II. Title: C-monkeys.

PS8615.O4376G36 2013 C813'.6 C2013-905163-5
C2013-905165-1

CHIZINE PUBLICATIONS
Toronto, Canada
www.chizinepub.com
info@chizinepub.com

Edited and copyedited by Brett Savory
Proofread by Samantha Beiko & Kelsi Morris

We acknowledge the support of the Canada Council for the Arts which last year invested $20.1 million in writing and publishing throughout Canada.

Published with the generous assistance of the Ontario Arts Council.

Printed in Canada

GAMIFICATION

"How many barrels will thy vengeance yield thee. . . ."

—Herman Melville

1

I had a wife. I had a daughter. I had a perfect little life. I developed an Internet gambling addiction. I'm still not comfortable calling it an addiction. That's what they want you to call it. But to me, the disease/recovery phrasing didn't capture the relationship between me and it, the precise nature of the self-destruct button I pressed again and again. Still, when the consequences arrived, I found myself (upon my hastily-met lawyer's advice) proclaiming that this addiction, this new companion I never knew I'd had, was the thing that actually made me do it. So I pleaded out, threw myself on the mercy of the court (and the mercy of my wife), agreed to whatever stipulations were made, and faced my stretch alone. What the lawyer didn't tell me (and after the worst was over, I never saw or heard from him again) was that the admission of addiction was to become my scarlet letter, the tattoo that stamped my transgression. Like being a registered sex offender, I was now an addicted Internet gambler.

The bargain for that admission had been assignment to an institution with a gambling

addiction program—something that would get me a reduction in time served. At least that's the reason my wife and I decided to take the deal. In the end, the transfer to an institution with a program didn't happen because no one or no entity with any influence—lawyer, wife, former colleagues, corrections bureaucracy—gave a shit once my case had been closed. Over time, I came to believe the deal was made, that the game had been played, with other motives entirely. The gambling excuse seemed to make everyone happier. My wife moved on, and legally changed my daughter's last name once I signed over full custody. My company wiped me off its books. Former colleagues could point to the admission and say, *Here's what happened and why*. It helped them move on, too. Yes, everyone was happier except me, serving my sentence. I was the addict. I was the fool. Post-incarceration, I was required to find my own program to meet the conditions of parole, to keep up the charade. So I endured the sessions and the groups, and talked the talk, and proclaimed that all my strength came from the Higher Power, and I learned to present myself like a lifelong drunk, one swallow of scotch from swirling back down the drain. I would even nod humbly whenever some sanctimonious lowlife warned me about the ceaseless dangers of temptation.

But none of this was true. Once I'd lost everything—wife, daughter, job, home, self-respect—I also lost the urge to gamble. True gamblers go back for more. I never had the desire again. The path that resulted from my gambling

was radically different than the path I'd been on, but the gambling itself was irrelevant. I think of it as the inciting incident. Really, it could have been anything. Vehicular homicide. Arson. Murder. Rape. Name your shame. Gambling was simply the kick that dislodged me from my perch and sent me plummeting to the bottom. Other circumstances, larger economic and social ones, kept me there, and that's what led me to accept Kiedler's offer.

Kiedler had been my protégé, back in that other life, when I was the director of employee development for Xcelsion—the Fortune 50 integrated energy producer. Before the move and the heavy cuts, Xcelsion had a global employee count somewhere between forty- and forty-five thousand. Basically, that meant a lot of development. I did some of the coaching and assessment myself and hired consultants to do the rest of the work, seeding the contracts between outside firms and the occasional over-priced thought leader with a best-selling book. I wrote reports and made the business case between productivity, human development, and performance. It was all bullshit—the theories, the correlations, the psychology—but I was good at it, the personnel decisions, the succession strategies, the leadership paths. I liked being a problem solver and a change agent. I liked having a budget and a team. I liked travelling to the business units, research labs, and refineries to meet management types and win them over with my quick understanding of their HR needs and my soft-sell explanation of how our

expertise could help them. I liked pitching the top executives and emerging from the firestorm of their scrutiny with a renewed mandate to turn our 19th-century widget-makers into 21st-century knowledge workers. I liked that no one really knew what any of it meant.

I didn't hire Kiedler, but I spotted his talent. He was a younger, less cynical version of me, and he thought all of my ideas were outstanding and he was energetic in pursuing whatever action steps I decided we should take. When he came to our family-hosted barbeques and Christmas parties, he would pitch in and help as though he were my Boy Friday even outside work. While I considered him bright enough to go places, and gave him glowing performance reviews, secretly, and in conversation with my wife, I couldn't decide whether his earnestness would help or hinder him in climbing the ladder. Part of me thought he was unlikely to go places because he lacked a devious nature.

As it happened, I was wrong about that, too.

He found me working in a call centre for benefits claims in Eau Claire, Wisconsin. I had altered my name so it was no mean feat reaching me, let alone navigating the call tree to my exact cubicle. I wondered if he'd hired someone to find me, or known someone who knew someone in the industry, or just followed the ghostly marks of the digital traces that are left behind no matter how lightly you live. I answered the phone and asked in friendly call-centre banter for the name of the person to whom I was

speaking, and heard someone chuckling instead. I couldn't decide whether the laughter was directed at me, or indifferent to me, and then the person on the other end spoke.

"Frank Reade, it is incredibly good to hear your voice."

I had only recently begun to call myself Frank Reade so this added to my confusion. I'd been Reid Frank back at Xcelsion, in my other life, and no one who knew my voice in a nostalgic sense would have used the new name. Nevertheless, it was clear that whoever was calling knew me from back then, knew me now, and had tracked me down like a fugitive. The world got a little lighter, the way it had that afternoon in my office when I'd realized I was about to be arrested. I looked at the script taped to my cubicle wall and stared at the ready-made phrases. *I'm sorry for your frustration. Is there any other help I can provide you with today? We're here twenty-four-seven to answer any questions you have.* None of it applied.

I reminded myself to breathe.

"It's Kiedler," the voice said. "Frank. No kidding. It's good to reach you."

And once he announced himself, I could almost see Kiedler standing before me. The only thing I didn't recognize about his voice was the confidence in it, but that's what happens when you leap-frog a half dozen levels in a few quick years. After my departure from the company, though not soon enough to divert the attention I got or blunt the punishment I received, a kick-back scandal had ripped through the

executive ranks like a case of Spanish Flu. The CEO, who'd only been on the job for slightly longer than me, got thrown out with his entire executive team—men and women I'd known fairly well. Those not infected were left behind to usher in the new dawn. Some, like Kiedler, got asked to step into temporary roles far above their station. Then, they'd brought back the previous long-term CEO, Neville Moss, who'd retired over his own scandal after he'd been linked to an off-book subsidiary doing oil deals with Iran. I'd never met Moss but his persona had always haunted the organization like a deposed dictator. It didn't surprise me when one of his conditions for resuming command was that the company move its headquarters from the Midwest, where it had been based for sixty-eight years, to southern California, where Moss had bought an estate. I'd read somewhere that ninety percent of such corporate relocations had no strategic or economic value whatsoever but were done for the CEO's own convenience. Yet, despite the self-serving nature of the move, I also marvelled at its effectiveness in establishing Moss's absolute control. He wasn't resuming the top job in any diminished capacity; instead, it was obvious to everyone from Wall Street to Riyadh that a wounded company was crawling on its hands and fucking knees to him.

"Seriously, Frank, how are you?"

You'd never guess that I'd done time, or that a couple pension funds had been flattened after Xcelsion's entire executive team had resigned, or, for that matter, that the nation's economy was for shit

and that we were all hanging on by some collective holy fuck handle. Everything was great in Kiedler's world. How nice it was to be a true believer.

"You've been keeping yourself busy?" he asked.

I had absolutely no way to answer this question except by mirroring its banality.

"Sure," I said. "Busy as can be."

He sounded disappointed all of a sudden, as though worried that he was intruding. Maybe that was the way a guy like Kiedler indicated remorse, or maybe he was drunk at three in the afternoon and losing his train of thought. Could a Kiedler fall, too?

But Kiedler hadn't fallen.

"I've got a line on a project I thought you might be interested in, if you're not too busy."

It took me a moment to process the questions and doubts into anything worth saying.

"You're offering me work?" I asked.

He hesitated, and said, "No." The word brought a flush to my face. Of course Kiedler wasn't offering me work. How could he? Asking him that question only embarrassed us both. He probably wanted me to paint his fence or walk his dog. I'd done both since leaving prison.

"It would be great to catch up," he said, as though he knew now that he'd made a mistake and the only way to correct it was to make fake plans for lunch.

"I'm in Wisconsin," I said. "I don't get to California often."

"Why don't you give me your email address, and we'll catch up that way."

"Actually, I'm not allowed unsupervised Internet

time," I said, and looked at my watch. "For about another three months."

"Ah," he said, and coughed. "No email?"

"Not outside work. Not even a smart phone. Not that the judge even knew what those were at the time. Text messages are a grey area. But I'd rather not take the chance."

"Your sentence was stupid and harsh, Frank. A waste of talent. I always meant to tell you how sorry I was."

He might have, but he never did. No visits. No letters. Like the rest of them.

"Hey," I said, "I get a lot more reading done."

This was becoming ridiculous for both of us, but I felt like rubbing his nose in my predicament. I didn't even care that my co-worker in the next cubicle, a heavy ex-biker gone tea party Republican with tattoos and a ponytail, was clearly listening in.

"Well, give me your mailing address and I'll drop by some time when I'm passing through."

"The next time you're passing through Wisconsin?" I asked.

He didn't respond. I wasn't supposed to give any personal information other than my first name to a caller, but in that moment I didn't give a shit.

So I gave Kiedler my address. An apartment over a trophy shop that was only open, far as I could tell, three or four days a month.

"Thanks," Kiedler said. "Well, Frank. Always a pleasure."

"Likewise," I said, and listened to him hang up. All of it, the whole cascade of anger and frustration

came over me then in a tsunami of regret, pain, and loneliness.

I clicked off for my lunch break and headed to the bathroom. Inside the stall, I threw up.

The call centre took up much of an old warehouse building that was located in the deep end of an industrial business park from the '70s. I'd found the job by chance. I'd gotten a new parole status that let me check in by phone rather than in person, and permission to cross state lines, so I'd left Minneapolis and headed East, thinking Chicago, maybe New York, some place to start a new life. The car broke down halfway across Wisconsin and I didn't have enough money to get it fixed so I looked for work instead. Luckily, there was actually work to find.

One of the things I liked to do on my lunch break was sit in my car and breathe. The parking lot behind the warehouse was fringed by forest. But just beyond the tree line was a gun range. No one had warned me about this, even jokingly. It was one of those quirky things I discovered on my own, and when I realized that the sound of shooting wasn't in my head, and that it was coming from the local chapter of the Wisconsin Wild Life Club and not an employee gone postal or an attack from Canada, I could not help but appreciate the juxtaposition of workplace and firing range. All office parks should have one.

Every minute or so, a shot rang out. I'd take a breath. Look at the trees swaying in the breeze

like seaweed. Hear the bang. Flinch up. Let the breath go. No matter how I readied myself for the sound, I always twitched with each retort and the bullet whistling by. Somehow, it made everything a little bit better. It was like yoga or a spa, only less ridiculous.

That afternoon, I needed it. It rocked me to hear from my old life. I'd achieved a kind of dull stasis after moving to this middle of nowhere. I was learning how to deal with what my mistakes had cost me, the calculus of loss. I breathed in. I watched the trees. I flinched with a shot and let the breath go. Then I looked over to see my colleague, the ex-biker from the cubicle next door, standing by my passenger side window. He rapped on the glass.

We'd never spoken outside of work before, but some barrier had been broken, no doubt, when he overheard my personal call. I reached across and popped the lock from the inside. Nobody locked anything in Eau Claire. City habits die hard.

"Mind if I get in?" he asked.

"Of course not," I said.

I wondered if he was going to offer me weed or proposition me for man-sex or suggest we go get a beer after work. He struggled to wedge his girth inside. All of his weight had collected in his stomach, an impressive gut that almost reached the glove compartment.

"Shit day, huh," he said, when he finally spoke.

I agreed wholeheartedly and nodded, but when I spoke, a much cheerier tone emerged. "No worse than some. You know how it is." My call centre voice.

"I know, brother, I know."

I noted the word *brother*. I'd seen a crucifix on the chain around his neck, *Jesus* written on his bicep, and a picture of the saviour taped to the side of his computer at work. Was I going to get the speech?

"I heard your personal call today," he said, awkwardly indirect to my ears.

"Sorry about that," I said.

He shrugged, as if it was understandable, just an embarrassing matter that needed to be discussed for my own good.

I wished I could appreciate the camaraderie, but mostly I just wanted to be alone. And yet, despite my exhaustion, I felt some urge to explain—by which I mean lie.

"It was the weirdest thing. Guy calls me to ask about his health plan, he recognizes my voice, and it's a friend from my old job. What are the odds?"

In other words, I didn't call out, they called in. I doubt the ex-biker believed me.

"You seem to be doing pretty well at this job," he said. "But I bet you got a lot on the line, a lot to lose, if you don't mind my saying."

I stared back, taking in the tattoos and the gut and the ponytail.

"What do you mean? And what's your name, by the way?"

"Cal. Cal Hardy."

The bang of a shot. I flinched. Cal didn't. A hunter. A vet. A bad-ass to my candy-ass. I let me breath out.

"What do you mean, Cal? You mind explaining what you're talking about?"

"You got this car. You got an apartment in town. You dress like a business man."

A business man? Khaki chinos I'd bought for fourteen dollars at Wal-Mart, a short-sleeve shirt with a collar. I thought it was the minimal in casual work wear but to Cal it made me look like management. The apartment in town. Jesus Christ. It didn't have a working stove and the refrigerator leaked a puddle onto the floor every night. The car was a nine-year-old Honda Civic with 200,000 miles that a friend's sister had off-loaded onto me because the resale was too low to bother with.

"I think we're all doing what we can to get by, aren't we, Cal? Nobody's getting rich."

He looked doubtful. I knew I didn't sound like anyone else he worked with, and I didn't dress like them, and I didn't fit in. Maybe Cal and the others thought I was an executive on some reality TV show, masquerading as an employee. Maybe I was the one who really owned the place, not the energetic Mr. Grady who gave a pep talk once a month to the "team."

"Your call today was definitely not acceptable," Cal said, a little edge in his voice. I breathed out, feeling hassled. An ex-biker stickler for rules.

"Well, like I explained, it was unexpected and not my fault. File it under random shit out of my control, right?"

Apparently, this was not right for Cal.

"You gave out your address," he insisted. "Guy got fired for doing that last month."

"Who's going to know, Cal?" I asked. "Besides you and me?"

"Calls are recorded. All of them."

"Yeah, but unless they knew which particular call to listen to, it would be a pretty arbitrary piece of bad luck for me if anyone ever happened on it, right?"

Of course, I knew all about arbitrary bad luck.

"I could tell them," Cal said.

I tried not to show any reaction.

"And why would you do that?"

I was curious. Our cards were on the table now, where I liked to see them.

"Better question is, why wouldn't I?"

"Okay," I said, "why wouldn't you tell them?"

He found some plastic schmutz on the dashboard to pick at, and avoided my gaze.

"I wouldn't tell them for a hundred dollars a month."

I sat back. Bang. Flinch. Breathe.

I needed the job, or some job. I had no more savings. I barely had gas money to get out of town. I was one bad day from being homeless. Cal might have guessed this. I guessed that Cal had done this before. Or maybe he was trying it out on a guy he figured deserved it, for being educated, for looking like a manager, for wearing fourteen-dollar khaki slacks, the kind you never needed to iron.

"Okay, Cal, I understand now," I said. "You mind if I get something out of the glove compartment?"

He looked suspicious but I reached over and opened the glove compartment, pressing it against his hard gut. Cal grabbed my wrist.

"Easy, Cal," I said, "just a piece of paper. Nothing dangerous."

In fact, in my other hand, the one closest to the door and out of Cal's sight, I had gripped the handle of a screwdriver, one I kept next to the seat because the lock sometimes needed jimmying for me to extract myself from the car. It was an old prison trick—do something suspicious but probably innocent in one direction while setting yourself up in the other. I didn't want to drive the screwdriver into Cal's eye socket, but I still felt the need to be prepared.

In any event, Cal did not give me reason to do so. He released my wrist and I slammed the glove compartment shut.

I showed Cal an envelope on which I'd scribbled some words.

"What's that?" he asked.

"A few notes I took," I said. "I've got the full record at home, but I thought you'd get the picture if I showed you some of the details."

"What details?"

"Let's see," I said, and peered closer. "Can't read my own damn handwriting. But on August second, around nine a.m., you told a caller to go fuck himself."

I looked up at Cal, then back down to the paper.

"On August fourth, around two-thirty, you asked a customer if she liked it like that, and you told her, 'Yeah, baby, you could ride me all day.'"

I grinned at that one.

"On August twenty-seventh, twenty-eighth, and twenty-ninth, you had half-hour calls in which you talked about survivalism, the supremacy of the white race, and the need to secure our borders. Are

you an Aryan Brotherhood kind of guy, Cal?"

"We have the right to protect what's ours."

"No argument from me, friend. And on September ninth, around ten A.M., you had a fifty-minute call, approximately, in which you talked about the Packers' defensive line and asked about the point spreads in the final pre-season game."

I was particularly impressed that anyone would bet on a pre-season point spread.

I handed Cal the envelope. "You can keep this if you like. I got notes at home."

It wasn't true, but I knew I'd remember the details.

"You get what I'm saying, Cal?" I asked.

My heart was beating, not in a fearful way, just a bit too much anger coming up all in a rush. Poor Cal wasn't to blame, but that didn't mean I'd let myself be pushed around. You learned how to stand your ground in prison.

"I get it," Cal said. He paused, as if uncertain what to say next, and finally shrugged. "Should we head back in? Lunch break is almost over."

Just like two pals on a break. It was my turn to shrug. We both got out of the car and trudged across the parking lot, leaning into the cold. Once we were inside, Cal said, "Oh, I forgot to mention, we got a team meeting in the conference room right at one. That's what I came out to tell you."

Nothing about trying to extort me. No, that hadn't been in his plans at all.

I followed Cal along the hall, a little warily, wondering if he had something else nasty in mind, maybe a blind corner where he could beat the shit

out of me. I did not have my screwdriver now. The cheap carpet and thin walls reminded me of one of the temporary administrative buildings at the prison. We reached the door and Cal hesitated and crouched down to tie his shoe. "Meeting's probably started," he said. "You go ahead."

Why are you tying your shoe? I thought. I stepped past him and put my hand on the door knob, said, "Fuck it" under my breath, and swung the door open.

The sudden strafing of flying objects, the strips of paper and floating orbs of colour, the cacophony of shrieks, was the explosion I'd been waiting for all along.

"Happy Birthday!"

Ex-biker grinning among them.

They threw a lunch-time party for everyone in the company on their birthday. Mr. Grady always made a point of showing up. I didn't remember that it was my birthday. But that was because I'd made up the date on my employment application.

Grady shook my hand now and thanked me for my great work, even as Cal pointed at me and laughed. "Look at his face! He never suspected a GD thing!"

It wasn't the gambling I liked, it was the risk of loss. At Xcelsion, I developed low self-esteem, according to my counsellor in prison, and some very self-destructive habits. A bit of it was personal—the marriage wasn't working, sex had stopped after our daughter was born, just stopped. But most of it was work-related. Ambivalence was a no-no in a

company that was so muscular in its pro-business, pro-oil stance. I was tired of faking it for sixty-five hours a week. Unlike Kiedler, I was not a true believer, just a guy doing a high-level job for a salary. Gambling filled the emptiness. I limited myself to online games played only at work. For some reason, the urges only arose when I was at the office. Maybe I was more afraid of getting caught at home than I was about getting caught at work. Certainly, I felt more safe at work than I did with my wife. I was, however, not careless or stupid about my vice. And I don't think it would have grown to any extent without the encouragement of a computer technician named Meeks. One day, working on my laptop in my office to install a new security system, he showed me a trick that would help me nullify it. I was amazed by how naturally and casually this conversation came up between us. He must have sensed my need the way a bartender recognizes the mood of a customer.

"It's called the Indonesian Exclusion," Meeks said, "in ode to the shit-hot spoofing they do over there."

There was dirt under his fingernails and his ponytail was greasy. He typed in some code which blackened my screen for a moment before it blinked back to life.

"What the fuck was that?"

"Notice the difference?"

"No," I said.

"Exactly," he announced. There was pride in his voice, like he'd proven his point. I still did not

understand what point he was trying to prove.

"As far as the security system is concerned, everything is normal, and no one who came in here would ever know the difference. You are, by all appearances, still logged in as you. But you're actually logged in as a duplicate you, in a duplicate system. Multiple duplicate systems, actually, but I don't want to get too technical."

"Meaning what?" I asked.

"Meaning you leave no digital traces of whatever you do from this point forward until you log out again and log back on to your original system. Basically, it's a series of false portals that cover your digital trail."

"Okay," I said. "Cool."

I never knew how to talk with technical guys, how to engage in a way that didn't make me feel foolish and out of my depth. Part of me was amazed he would tell me this. I was a VP, not a temp. I could have him fired. That dissonance kept me off balance, or maybe it was just my curiosity, the itch to press a button.

It was clear to Meeks, however, that I still didn't get it.

"Meaning you can do whatever you want now," trying to impress upon me the power of what he was showing. "You can explore any website you want, write any email to anyone you want, and nothing will be traced to this computer and your log-in ID. You can shit all over a customer on a chat site, and no one will know who you are or be able to prove it was you. You can do a deep data search on anyone

you want, your boss, your potential hire, the hot little temp you want to see naked. You can bet on the Superbowl coin toss. I wrote the code myself. They spent millions on a jacked up security program and I beat it without even staying up late."

He wrote the URL and password down for me. Told me to memorize it and destroy the paper. I asked him why he was showing me the end-around. He shrugged.

"I don't know. I guess I'm a pirate at heart. Doesn't it drive you nuts how much we're being watched?"

"Here?" I asked. "At the company?"

He shrugged again. "Here. There. Everywhere. Someone always has their finger up your ass."

"Right," I said.

I made a point about mentioning the potential benefits of leaving some nasty comments about competitors some time. But Meeks was either not impressed, knew I was lying, or had already mentally moved on.

"Good," he said. "Glad I could help bring a little evil into the world."

After he'd left, I visited a website I'd heard about but never had the courage to check out, and placed a bet on a World Cup soccer match between Ghana and Japan.

You can bet on anything today, anywhere in the world. We're living in a gambling golden age. There's something outlandish and rebellious about betting on events that are utterly unconnected to your life. Who cares about a Formula One race in Monaco or a cricket test in Bermuda or a kick-boxing bout in

Bangkok? Who cares if a butterfly in China flaps its wings? But when you gamble, everything becomes interesting. You have a stake in just being alive.

The problem: instead of dealing with one or two bookies who will break your legs for not paying up, you're locking into algorithmic labyrinths that suck your account every time you play. Before long, you've blown past your pre-determined risk threshold, just like one of those Wall Street assholes who hedges the firm's entire value on a house of cards.

That's when the game changes.

I lost a lot of money fast. A few months later, Meeks showed me how to keep playing.

The morning after Kiedler called, a UPS delivery man stood at my door in brown pants and shirt. Dressed in my white underwear and t-shirt, still groggy from the half bottle of Southern Comfort I'd drank to stop my brain for a while, I explained that he had the wrong address. I had never received so much as a post card at my apartment before. But he showed me my name—my new name—on the sheet, and I signed. I was suspicious of the contortion of the envelope he handed me, a little pudge in the middle indicating that papers, forms, or whatever legal documents being sent were not the only contents. I did not recognize the sender's name. I figured it was my wife's latest lawyer, but what more could she take from me? I was almost curious what she might do next. Alone, next to the kitchen sink and a window where a small house plant had been left behind by a previous tenant, I opened the envelope

and found a thin cell phone, a credit card, and a California driver's license with my new name. There was a Post-it note on the cell phone screen with a phone number written on it.

I dialed the number and Kiedler answered. He said it would be better if we talked that way, off-line so to speak, about the job he had in mind.

He told me I was uniquely suited to the task. In fact, he was certain that no one was more qualified for it or better positioned to take it on. That made me worth my weight in dollars. What he meant was, how many other ex-executive ex-cons who'd dropped out of existence and changed their names had my background in personality testing, human development, and change agenting? What he said was, "Who else knows Xcelsion as well as you, gets its culture, knows the pressure points, and understands on a personal level the panic that can overcome a successful person when they stand on the knife edge of failure and disgrace?" Who else, I agreed. I reminded him, because I was wondering about his sanity by this point, that I'd been fired by Xcelsion, that there were probably laws against hiring me for anything, on even a contractual basis. He assured me that our arrangement would be strictly off book and no one at Xcelsion who ever knew me was around anymore anyway.

Not a big commitment, he continued, or any personal risk. Short time-frame, big pay-off. A little travel. A lot of brain power. No trace of activities. He added that he saw this as a new beginning and

told me he had a feeling that the kind of work he had yet to describe was more valuable than I might realize, not just to Xcelsion, where the problems were relatively contained to one isolated though significant issue, but to other companies as well. "All organizations go through this kind of turmoil," he said, and added, "It's human nature." He told me he could see me becoming a specialty contractor, some kind of McKinsey/CIA hybrid consultant, because of my unusual resume. Covert was a growth segment in the global consulting industry.

I asked him how much. It was really the only question that mattered. He offered me a year's salary—my old salary—a figure I would never have imagined possible.

"Off book?" I repeated.

"Wired anywhere you want," he said, and then added, gratuitously I thought, "to any name you choose."

2

In San Diego, I was put up in a suite on the thirty-second floor of one of the dozen hotels overlooking the marina. Isolated in luxury, far from my trophy apartment in Wisconsin, I felt lost. I watched CNN. I ordered room service. I did my old prison regimen of push-ups, sit-ups, and calisthenics, five times a day. I spent too much time calculating loss and wondering what Kiedler had in mind. I waited for his call.

On the third morning, assuming I'd been forgotten, I tried Kiedler's number, still uncomfortable handling a cell phone, even one not traceable to me. When there was no answer, I left my room in shorts and a t-shirt and went for a long walk along the sandy breakwater, feeling as though I'd escaped from a mental institution. I'd forgotten the phone, I realized halfway to the point, but I didn't care. Phones that haven't been ringing when you hold them don't suddenly ring as soon as you leave them behind. Except, of course, they do, and when I got back to the room I saw a missed call and

two texts. Kiedler wondering where I'd gone. Kiedler wanting to see me immediately.

"The reason I reached out to you," Kiedler began, when we met at a dockside restaurant for an early lunch, "is that Neville's in a jam."

In spite of everything, it impressed me to hear Kiedler speaking about Neville Moss, the CEO of Xcelsion, as though he were Kiedler's close friend.

"What do you mean by a jam?" I asked.

"He had an affair," Kiedler said.

I wasn't shocked but felt I should act that way so I spent a moment looking out at the seagulls beyond the railing bobbing like mobiles on string.

"It's insane," Kiedler agreed. "You should meet Neville's wife. She's a force of nature. Intelligent. Beautiful. Thirty years younger. What more could he need?"

I shrugged. "Tenderness maybe?"

"I don't know," Kiedler said. "I think it's more complicated than that. There's a lot of interesting research recently on brain chemistry in executives, how much it changes over the life span of a career. Men become more reflective, more sentimental. Women actually get more aggressive. We're starting to incorporate that in our coaching process. Someday we'll be able to anticipate most of these interpersonal derailers, I bet."

I felt his pause go on for too long, and assumed he was thinking about me and my own brain chemistry, whatever had happened there.

"So he had an affair," I said. "Why's that the end

of the world? Are you worried about a harassment lawsuit or just bad PR?"

Kiedler seemed to appreciate my getting down to business. "The problem is," he began, "you don't slide on affairs anymore. Not like you used to. Not when you're a CEO. It's not about whatever morals clause may be in the contract. Every time a CEO goes down for an affair it's because someone gains. Boeing. HP. Best Buy. It doesn't matter how big you are. Those were precision strikes aimed at removing someone that someone else felt needed to be removed."

Still a true believer. Back in the day, I would have said something about his paranoia but I needed to play along.

"So someone's trying to oust Neville?"

Kiedler stirred his drink, a club soda, and looked out at the seagulls. He was sweating lightly and he looked like shit. I was fitter than I'd been seven years ago, thanks to prison.

"It's part of the game, isn't it?" he said. "Oust him. Pressure him into some deal he doesn't want to do. Reduce his stature and authority. Or maybe the objective is to knock Xcelsion back down now that we're finally on our feet again. We have enemies. Neville has enemies. Of course he does. And he has made himself and us completely vulnerable. The woman in question is an executive at one of our smaller competitors, a natural gas producer out of Houston called Chapek Energy. Yes. I know. Unbelievable. We never paid them any attention before this, except maybe as an acquisition target. Neville claims he didn't know she was in the

business when the affair started. Is he telling the truth? It's actually possible but it looks terrible. And how could she not know who she was sleeping with? He's Neville Moss! Was she trying to influence him? Steal some information? If you made up stuff like this, threw it into a novel, no one would believe you. It's Fifty Shades of John le Carré."

"Who knows about the affair?" I asked, showing suitable concern. "A lot of people? A few?"

"I think it's a containable number. Neville's secretary approached me when she became suspicious. She's completely trustworthy. She'd never embarrass Neville. To the best of my knowledge, no one else in the company knows. I can't go to our security with this. I can't even go to an outside problem-solving entity. Given our history, the slightest whiff will have the Justice Department all over us. The Board's solid for now, with everything going full throttle, but you know they probably resent Neville the way he bends them over. One excuse and they'll put in their own guy. You want a coffee?"

I did not want a coffee. Kiedler did not want a coffee. The waitress smiled and left us. She wore short white shorts, and a blue sailor's shirt.

"What's the status of the affair right now?" I asked. "Is it active? Are they meeting in public places?"

"I'd like to say it's over," Kiedler said, "that we're cleaning up something after the fact. But that's not quite true. They haven't met in three or four months, thank God. But he emails and texts her all the time. Can you imagine Neville texting someone?"

I couldn't. I found it hard to imagine Neville Moss, the industry icon, as a real person.

"How did they meet in the first place, some industry event?"

"At a wellness centre. Neville's health had been under par. He needed to unplug for a bit. Recharge his batteries. So we stayed away while he was there. That was a mistake. I think he didn't know what to do with himself."

"So people at the wellness centre would know about this?"

"Maybe. But they're extremely discreet. This wasn't a Club Med in Acapulco. It's a highly exclusive resort."

"Why was she there?"

"Good question. You see where I'm going? That's why I suspect she was put in his way for a reason."

"And since then?"

"As far as I can tell, no meetings or physical contact. Neville has been fully engaged. We're very active with deal-making right now, rolling up acquisitions, properties, and lines. He hasn't been out of my sight for the past few months. I've checked his mobile call log and I don't think they've talked, just texts and emails."

"So where do I come in?"

Kiedler twisted in his chair and grimaced.

"I need you to get inside Neville's head, get a clear sense for how he thinks and what he'd do in unusual circumstances. You've always had that knack for figuring out top executives. You're the best I've ever seen. Don't worry, I can get you close enough to secure what you need."

A hundred worries came to mind but I focussed on the one that seemed most important in the moment.

"To what end?"

Kiedler smiled. "You once told me that every crisis or problem has a narrative. That the way people perceive a threatening event and talk about it impacts the value that can be extracted from it. And that if we shape the narrative one way rather than another, we can get the results we prefer. Do you still believe that?"

Was Kiedler asking me whether I believed in anything I'd said back then?

"Of course I do," I answered. And I realized, in that moment, that I did believe in that, maybe always would. It was perhaps the one truth I could believe in. The mind is linear but life is chaos. We're susceptible to narratives that explain away the confusion, reduce the noise. I'd used the concept most deliberately during career pathing, helping push an executive with leadership potential up the ladder, organizing their experiences to maximize the learning we were after. We got so good at it, sometimes we'd throw an obstacle in their way just to see how they'd handle it, an urgent project, an impossible goal, and we'd use their responses as coaching lessons. Here's how you do it better. Here's what you need to become. We called it gamification because it allowed us to turn reality into a game with goals and rules of our choosing.

"You want me to game Neville Moss?" I said. The very idea made me wonder what Kiedler was up to, how far he actually wanted to go.

"I want you to game her," Kiedler said.

It took me a moment to understand who he meant.

I had never imagined, when Kiedler brought me on, that he'd intend for me to actually visit the Xcelsion offices, but he told me not to worry.

"Almost everyone you ever knew is gone."

To relieve my concerns, we went over the list of people I might run into. It amazed me how few names I recognized, how wholesale the changes had been. Only a half dozen or so were familiar.

"Those three are back in Minneapolis," Kiedler said. "Arrington works in Florida, Tim Leason in New York. Sarah Daniels is here but she never comes into the office, and I'll make sure she doesn't. Nobody does. Not on a daily basis. Only for special occasions. That's just the way it's done now."

Telecommuting had become real, apparently, during the past few years, and the advantage went to me. How could the world have changed so much in such a short period of time? After Kiedler left to go to the office and meet with Neville Moss, I spent the rest of the day on my balcony watching the Pacific, calculating loss.

The light shifted as the evening arrived. You think, when you're in Southern California, that a bright and beautiful day will have no end—until it does. My remorse emulsified as the darkness deepened. It mixed with anger.

What right did I have to be angry? It was even more ridiculous to feel anger not at myself, or my wife, or even at Meeks, but at Xcelsion; to hate the

company and what it did, which was not benign or enlightened but necessary. It only did what we needed it to do. Why not rage at a sunset or a rock?

I was still locked in that irrational mixture of remorse and anger when Kiedler showed up at my hotel room. I let him in. He looked shaken and worn out. I remembered that he'd planned to tell Neville Moss that he knew about the affair, that it had to stop, that he, Kiedler, needed to handle it discreetly. I remembered that my ability to contribute to Kiedler's plan depended completely on the outcome of that conversation. I was nervous suddenly, seeing Kiedler's despair.

"How'd it go?" I asked, cheerfully.

"Hardest thing I've ever done," he answered.

He went to the bar near the balcony and poured himself a healthy vodka over ice. I'd never known Kiedler to touch spirits before.

"How bad?" I asked, fearing Kiedler fired, my contract over.

"Bad," Kiedler answered. Then: "He's on board. He understands completely. I've got total access. We're good to go."

I was surprised by the news, and confused.

"Then what's the problem?"

Kiedler looked at me, his eyes darkly lined.

"I never thought I'd see Neville Moss cry."

"Oh," I said.

To me, it was the most unlikely of reactions. Apparently, the affair meant something to him after all.

I was surprised by the building, how out of place it seemed in the SoCal sun. The office in Minneapolis had been post-modern in design. No right angles, silver windows bending with the sweep of the bluff, river-facing, a sun-reflecting roof, self-irrigating grounds. The new Xcelsion HQ looked industrial or fortress-like, squat and broad, only five or six stories high, a block of concrete with vertical slit-like windows, a small logo with the definitive X, an enormous American flag, a cluster of cameras at the security gate.

Kiedler must have read my mind.

"We're leasing. It's the old Groves Corporation, like Rand, but for energy policy instead of nuclear missiles. Coincidentally, that was Neville's first job after military school, so this was like coming back to the place where he helped lobby energy policy in the '70s, laying the ground work for investment and deregulation decades before those ideas became mainstream. But one look and you understand: Anyone who says we moved out to San Diego to waste shareholder dollars on sunshine ought to get a tour. Neville believes you put every dime into asset growth, whether times are good or bad. I wish everybody in the company felt the same way."

Inside, it was less off-putting, more what I expected, though there was a throwback quality to the decor, lots of dark wood, lush carpets, wallpapered walls. I was nervous walking around. An elevator is an elevator. A desk is a desk. But the hush and the dark colours and the forbidding demeanour of the secretary, who must have been Nancy, was

more intimidating than I would have expected. Kiedler went inside to see Moss first and discuss a few items while I waited until Nancy finally nodded me in. I'd seen plenty of pictures of Moss before, in newspapers or magazines, but had never met him in person. He was much thinner than I'd expected, and frail, and he looked every one of his years. He leaned back from his desk, without a smile, without acknowledgement, as I entered.

"Neville, this is Frank Reade," Kiedler started. I took the open chair, and sat stiffly. "Neville is a visionary," Kiedler continued, as though he and I were alone and not sitting in front of the man. "When Neville took over Midwest Hastings twenty-four years ago, it was an unwieldy producer, in a mess of debt, slow to adapt, going nowhere. After the merger with Triumph, Neville doubled the value of Xcelsion every year until his hiatus and he's got us back on that same pace again in the four years since he returned. Now we're top six among the vertically integrated. That's an unprecedented, completely unheralded rate of growth. Neville doesn't want the accolades. He's bigger than that. He wants the world to be better, to be more secure, and he has this core belief, well, I don't want to demean anyone, but there are a lot of Ayn Rand BSers among oil execs, and they all talk like they were wildcatters when they were young and still scrape tar sand off their cowboy boots before they go into work in the morning. Neville's not in it for the money or himself, he's in it for us, for all of us. And if he has to be a son of a gun sometimes, it's for

a purpose. This company has expanded from trucks, drill rigs, and pipelines to derivatives, networks, and relationships. It provides services no one would have imagined thirty years ago. But the entire energy industry needed a drastic overhaul. I always point out that we have not been through a real energy crisis in generations. Remember the '70s? Peak oil. The end of western economic growth. Now, we think three-buck gas is a national tragedy, and we don't think about shortages or gas lines or bottle necks or politics even as we've gone through twenty more or less continuous years of war in the Middle East with almost no net impact on quality of life. We're hugely, immensely better off, and we don't realize it, and it's due to a few men leading the world with a very old-fashioned sense of stewardship, Neville Moss first among them."

It was quite a speech, and Kiedler surprised the hell out of me. The Kiedler I'd known was into performance metrics and socio-psychology, not leadership greatness or industry trends. He'd molded into his new role like a thespian, or maybe I'd underestimated him badly back in the day.

"It's a story that needs to be told," I echoed, falling into line.

"Exactly," Kiedler answered, his face flushed, as though emotional. "I've told Neville we need him to write his autobiography. A blood and guts story. Weaving it in with the story of this industry. It's got to do what Churchill's histories did for his legacy, but with the added challenge that the events in question are largely unknown to the general public.

It's got to read like a novel and a history."

"War and Peace," I said, and saw Kiedler wince.

"Michener," Kiedler said. "The sweep, the change."

"A little Robert Ludlum maybe," Moss added. "Some Gadsen Wells or Ian Fleming if we want to have fun."

I could not help but grin at Moss contributing something so unexpected.

"Except we don't want to cheapen it," Kiedler said. I was surprised to hear him counter Moss. "We want this to be legacy stuff. Leave the melodrama to the Eichenwalds and Stewarts."

Kiedler was oddly animated in Moss's presence, leaning forward, lots of gesturing, less confident and at ease, more salesy, the jokes a little forced, as though Moss made him nervous. Even so, my old protégé was skillful. I could see him bringing Neville along. Not a yes-man, exactly, but a sharpener of perspective, a framer of issues. I watched Moss for any sign of approval or annoyance, and saw nothing. I wondered if Moss was the kind of man who needed the noise of argument around him to feel persuaded. I tried to imagine the conversation Kiedler and Moss must have had about Moss's affair.

"You up for this?" Moss asked me.

"Yes, sir," I said. Was the "sir" too much? Moss engendered that kind of military respect. "I'd love to help."

Kiedler took over. "You'll shadow Neville for the next few weeks, pump him for thoughts and insights. Meetings. Flights. Car rides. He'll even answer you through the bathroom door. What's

your calendar like this week, Neville? We have you going to Dubai, right?"

"That's cancelled. We're meeting next month in Zurich instead. Those guys are always in a better mood when they're closer to their money." Moss looked to me again. "Nothing's more boring than the life of a CEO."

"Kevin tells me it's an adventure every day," I said, feeling silly as soon as the words were out.

"I don't know why Kevin just doesn't work on this himself. No one knows me better."

A complaint in his voice. A discomfort. Kiedler broke in.

"I'll be co-piloting this, Neville, you know that. But I'm not a writer. This guy's done great work on other bios."

"Who'd you write for?" Moss asked.

"You know you can't ask that, Neville," Kiedler said. "He's got more NDAs than we do. Nothing worse than a ghostwriter telling stories."

"No," Moss said. "We don't want that. When do we start?"

If I was really Moss's biographer, I would have been in for a hell of a challenge. I could decipher him in only the crudest ways.

He had graduated from West Point, flown intelligence missions in Vietnam, interned at the Pentagon and the Department of Defense, and gotten his engineering degree at Stanford, but he was habitually late to everything. This surprised me. I'd expected military precision, an early riser, someone

who started and finished meetings on time. Moss as CEO, I came to see, was less a person than an entity, a resource, an oracle, approached from hundreds of directions at once. In the hallway, in the office, in the limo, every encounter brought with it a plea, a reminder, a push for attention, a request for reallocation, the offering of information that might spin or tilt a pending decision. Sometimes those executives were good-natured and collegial, once in a while desperate, even fearful. Moss was steady, but in subtle ways he played each exec, each request, differently. At a surface level, he was like a football coach, gruff, quick to anger, but his default mode was to overturn expectations at every opportunity. He was harsh when you expected camaraderie, surprisingly supportive when someone was worried or concerned. When he made a joke, it seemed to create enormous relief, a sense that everyone in the room was within the inner circle. When he got tough, it caused others to look sick. I saw this on my second afternoon, sitting in on a meeting that included nine executives, fourteen handlers, and three secretaries taking notes. One of the vice presidents was giving a report on a wind farm in Oklahoma. Suddenly, Moss leaned forward, started to respond, and stopped. His face purpled up as though he were choking or having a stroke. Moss glanced at the secretary, flailed his hand, and she immediately stopped typing on her laptop.

"This is how goddamn stupid we are," he said. "You've been telling me natural gas was over for years, and it was just beginning. And now we're up

to our nuts in alternative fucking energy and we may as well be shitting our money away."

"We're still sixty percent gas, Neville," the VP said. "It's a healthy mix."

"Are you kidding me?" Moss's hand came down hard. "We have left billions on the table. Billions. It makes me want to throw up. Do you want to know what alternative energy is? It's not clean energy, or feel-good energy, or wouldn't-it-be-nice energy. It's energy that you turn to when all the rest of the energy is too hard to get. Coal was alternative when we ran out of trees. Crude was alternative when we ran out of whales. Natural gas is the most important alternative in my lifetime, and we gave away twenty percent of our stake just to make ourselves look better on goddamn PBS and the *New York* Fucking *Times*."

He leaned back: "Clear the room."

The suddenness of the command froze everyone in place until it was understood, then everyone but the team of nine executives quickly gathered their phones and papers and rose to leave, me along with them. Whatever it was that couldn't be said in front of us, I never learned, but in the elevator an hour later Moss gave me a grim smile.

"I have a personal theory," he said, "that Jesus Christ was the world's first CEO."

"Oh?" I said. I offered nothing else because I thought I'd heard, at first, that Jesus Christ was the world's *worst* CEO, and what can you say to that?

"Yeah, you remember Jesus' retirement party. He gave himself piece by fucking piece to twelve guys

who couldn't run an organization without him."

I laughed, enough to show how witty he was but not so freely that he would think I was making fun. At another level, I knew exactly what he meant. The higher you rise in a company, the less personal life you have, the more you become one with the organization. By the time you reach the very top, the only way out is betrayal and crucifixion.

I had, by my third day, collected enough tics of conversation and habits of thought, enough of a sense of Moss's appetites and interests, to do a reasonable impression. At night, in the marina hotel room, I honed that impression by reading a few thousand of Moss's old emails and texts, logging onto a safe internal account where all that correspondence was stored. The emails to executives were notably terse, busy or dismissive. Only a few got personal in a stiff sort of way, thanking a report for giving his or her all, offering congratulations on some rite of passage, the birth of a son, the marriage of a daughter. Moss turned on a different voice when he wrote company-wide emails, sounding almost Patton-esque. At such moments, Moss liked to talk about the "adventure" and the "journey" and the critical difference employees were making, and the importance of teamwork and values and trust. The phrasing sounded inauthentic, and I wondered if Kiedler had written it. There were also a small number of work-related emails I filed to one side because they were strange or even disturbing, filled with rambling incoherent thoughts about particular

people or circumstances, so long-winded they seemed written while drunk. The external emails, on the other hand, were often awkwardly exuberant and cheerful, a bit like a grandfather trying too hard. Moss liked to forward tired Internet jokes to friends and often made comments specific to the recipient, "You'll love this, Don." The replies to Moss were always over the top, "I never laughed so hard! Where do you find this stuff?" I got the feeling Moss intimidated people in every facet of his life.

I was most interested in the emails to her, the woman I knew only as Amanda. Moss took more time with those messages, I could tell. Complete sentences, correct spelling, reasonable grammar. Boyish and eager to please. Consistent and highly responsive, one or two a day initiated by Moss, and every reply from her answered in turn within a few hours, unless it was the middle of the night. Moss came across as a love sick puppy, dancing around someone who was reluctant, maybe even indifferent to his interests. He tried too hard. There were naughty moments, nothing outrageous or raunchy, but embarrassing to read, an older man attempting to be intimate and sexy with a younger woman but flubbing it. Moss mentioned once that he envied the pendant she wore around her neck because it dangled occasionally between her breasts. He claimed that he wanted to drench her feet in champagne and suck her toes. This, I noticed, cross-referencing to a file of business emails, had taken place immediately after a major deal with ExxonMobil. I imagined what a reporter would be able to do with such a revelation,

how much ridicule could be wrung from the timing. Sometimes he expressed his genuine enthusiasm for other, non-sexual hobbies, like golf or sailing or reading cheap thrillers. He mentioned Ludlum a few times, Ian Fleming, Michael Crichton, and a couple others I hadn't heard of like Trevanian and Gadsen Wells. Amanda's replies were rarely direct, and she kept an emotional distance from Moss, maintained a little formality, almost as though he were her boss or mentor. Only rarely did she drift into the kind of contemplative wistfulness you see when one person pines for another in a greeting card sort of way. "I'm looking out the hotel balcony at the Gulf," she wrote a month earlier, "and I'm thinking of that sailing trip we talked about, and wishing you were close to me right now." Like a woman from a more chaste era allowing her true feelings to show. I felt dirty reading them, intrusive, mercenary, and I took my time with my first one, refining it over and over, cutting it to the bone, knowing I needed to get the pattern of send and reply up again soon or she would wonder what was wrong.

"Amanda, I'm so sorry I've been distracted. You wouldn't believe how busy I've been, how much weight I feel like I'm carrying sometimes. But I've been thinking of you, and hoping that you still think about me, even if it's only once in a while. I yearn to hear from you."

Yearn was the risk. Old-fashioned. Awkward. But maybe telling. If Moss, the Moss of the earlier emails anyway, wanted Amanda to know he really meant it, he was the kind to throw in a word that

was suffused with sincerity, drenched in meaning. Yearn.

I hit send, using Moss's private account, which had been closed to other traffic. I texted Kiedler and told him it was on.

Kiedler texted back within seconds. "I saw it go by. It's perfect."

An hour later, I got my first reply from Amanda.

"I know what you mean about weight."

I upped the cadence from the start. I emailed her three times a day, texted another four or five. I don't know why. Some instinct, I suppose. The feeling that I had the hot hand. Or maybe I was just lonely. Having revisited the familiar territory of self-loathing, I wanted to roll in it.

I made sure, whenever I wrote to her, that I incrementally upped the stakes, too. I began to reveal details that should never have been let out of the corner office, stuff that could affect share price, even oil and gas futures. All of it was made up. I tried to hew closely to current events while interpreting them incorrectly or randomly, so that there was plausibility to what I was writing, but nothing that could match any internal memos or memories of what had been said in meetings by whomever. When I allowed Moss to get intimate in those emails or texts, I pressed Amanda on her love for him, asking for more clarity, more commitment, while playing randomly, bizarrely, with Moss's strange obsession for her feet and breasts. (Once, after a particularly heated series of emails to her,

I masturbated furiously, and felt strange and mentally unhealthy afterwards, locked in my luxury suite.) I let Moss talk about his feelings for her, his longing to be closer, and tried to prompt or provoke her into reassurances by expressing subtle doubts and insecurities, even dismissing the viability of their relationship because of the difference in ages, the impossibility of circumstances. Amanda was not easily led. She was hesitant in a very artful way. She pirouetted around commitment and all leading questions. She rarely even acknowledged what was being asked of her. The most direct response she'd ever given was the first one. "I know what you mean about weight." Somehow that had hit a mark which every other comment or plea missed.

At least fifty percent of the emails were impossible for Moss to have written. I coordinated with Moss's calendar and preset the release timing to occur during meetings or other easily referenced and reliably witnessed events. Five of the emails I sent, scattered judiciously through the first week's stream of correspondence, served as blatant red flags. Two, for example, were written at the exact time that Moss was with nine other energy executives as well as former President Bush and the new Crown Prince of Saudi Arabia. The event was actually covered by CNN, a walk across the grass at the Presidential library in Texas, a wave to the press. Another took place while Moss was unconscious and having dental surgery. He had extremely sensitive teeth, apparently, and could only be treated while completely under, a state of indisposal that required

the signing of a letter of temporary transfer of power, addressed to the Board, but never delivered, a CYA measure insisted upon by the General Counsel.

Each time Amanda responded to an implausible email, she helped craft an alternative narrative. The affair had never happened. Neville Moss had never participated. There was evidence that Moss could not even have sent a good percentage of the emails that had been part of their correspondence. This nullified or at least undermined any claim she might potentially make to a long-standing affair. Create questions and confusion, give journalists doubts, make them timid about repeating unverifiable or dubious facts, provide friendly pundits and opinion columnists enough leverage to deride her character, even her sanity, portray her as another slutty nut. This was the groundwork that was being laid.

At some level, it was easy. At another, it wore me down. A strategy that seemed reasonable in theory, even intriguing, felt sordid and corrupt in the doing. I was glad, for once, that I did not have to face anyone at the end of the day, smile, give a kiss, knowing inside what I was involved with.

Hi, honey, how was work today?

Same old same old. I destroyed someone.

"Don't get sentimental," Kiedler said to me on the phone that evening when I expressed my first doubts. "If there's even a one percent chance that she's trying to undermine Neville or the company, we have to play to that scenario."

After eleven days in, it didn't seem that way to me. As far as I could tell, she was innocent of all

suspicion. If so, her involvement with Neville Moss was truly bad luck. It didn't matter that she had been pursued in a one-sided way and had never propagated or encouraged the relationship, Kiedler wanted her reputation destroyed and he was paying me a lot of money to do it.

I didn't even know her last name. I only knew that she worked for a small competitor, an acquisition target. I couldn't remember the name of that company. I searched widely for any cross-reference between Xcelsion and a small nat gas producer but found nothing. What would my old judge, the one who'd banned me from unsupervised Internet time and cell phones, think if he could see me now? Two months before my parole was finished, I spent much of my days and most of my nights prowling the nether world.

I didn't want to ask Kiedler directly. I worried that he would view my interest as more personal than professional, that he would see cracks forming where no cracks should be. He would be wary of me, given my demise. He *should* be wary of me. But that evening the name of her company came to me, unbidden, via CNN. I had the TV on most of the time, but the sound always off. The flicker of images, the presence of faces, allowed me to feel ever so slightly less alone. The graphic of a deep-sea drilling platform on the TV screen caught my attention, and I found the remote and turned up the volume.

"We're still trying to figure out what happened to that drilling rig that exploded and sank in the South

Pacific in the aftermath of the earthquake that measured 7.6 on the Richter Scale," the announcer said. It was that grim but cheerful voice used to describe some horrific but distant catastrophe. "This video was taken by a French family on their yacht about eight hundred miles from Tahiti in the region of the Rui Nodo archipelago."

I watched, my own curiosity piqued. A green, forested island in the distance with a blunt conical mountain in the centre surrounded by an aquamarine sea. The image was so still it might have been a photograph until a shiver rippled over everything and a convulsive shaking made me feel slightly ill. The light changed, not from clouds, but a strange distortion to the air, like film stock emulsifying or a distant explosion brightening the sky, the sea itself changing after that, tinting up, turning into wine, growing choppy, as though disturbed from below.

"The anonymous environmental activist group, Carbon Audit, is claiming, however, that a natural earthquake was not to blame at all. Instead, they're saying that the Rui Nodo archipelago was the site of experimental deep-sea hydraulic fracturing. That's the process, commonly known as fracking, used to extract natural gas or shale oil trapped within layers of subterranean rock. Carbon Audit claims that the gas producer, Chapek Energy, has been using this experimental technique in the vicinity, but they're also claiming that Chapek is operating under the direction of energy giant Xcelsion. These are unsubstantiated claims, of course, and we are merely reporting the Carbon Audit public statement.

We have reached out to both Xcelsion and Chapek Energy but have yet to obtain any comments from spokespersons at either of those corporations."

"Is that possible, John? Could deep-sea fracking be responsible for this kind of devastation?"

"In terms of magnitude, Alan, it would be unprecedented. And I emphasize this is pure speculation. But there have been unproven instances in the continental US when hydraulic fracturing has been linked to seismic activity."

"Thank you, John. We'll check in when we get more details about this important environmental story."

Chapek Energy. That was the company Kiedler had mentioned, the one that had been on no one's radar screen. I muted the TV and called Kiedler. It was past nine o'clock. It occurred to me as I waited that I didn't know if he was married, had kids, lived like a monk or in a castle. I knew nothing about Kiedler's personal life. But I did know that he'd been less than candid about the relationship between Chapek and Xcelsion. He answered on the second ring.

"I was just watching this thing on CNN," I explained.

"Tell me about it. That's all we've been dealing with for three days."

"They're saying Chapek Energy is drilling for Xcelsion?"

"Carbon Audit is saying that, and the fine journalists at CNN are only too happy to parrot it, early and often."

"So it's not true?"

A silence.

"This is the way Carbon Audit works."

"Who are they? I've never heard of them."

"I keep forgetting you've been away from the Internet."

And in prison.

"Carbon Audit is like WikiLeaks. They're anonymous hackers that specialize in releasing the confidential documents of energy companies. A few years ago they exposed BP's own internal documents on Deep Water before they could be scrubbed. They do this thing on their website where they track all offshore drilling activity on an interactive Google satellite map and red-dot leased assets specifically because they believe big oil outsources the dirty work. It's all BS of course, the sort of data visual that makes a corporation look as though it's hiding something. But I know for a fact that the rig they claim we leased to Chapek is getting worked on in Malaysia right now."

I felt like an amateur for sounding so suspicious.

"So why are they making the claim?"

"Because they can. Because all we can do is offer milquetoast rebuttals three weeks after they've been worked over by ten lawyers in general counsel. They're already making noise about the extinction of some rare lizard as a result of this disaster, and I bet it will be their mascot before this is over. It's really just a form of social media blackmail. As soon as we fund the right researchers, all of whom are probably Carbon Audit cronies, put together some blue ribbon panel of coral reef experts, and throw some million dollar stipends around, this whole

thing will go away. My biggest worry is that Neville will be too stubborn to play that game."

"Chapek is the company she works for, right?"

"Correct. But Chapek's not the issue," Kiedler said. "Focus on her."

"Of course," I answered. I knew better than to push him any further, but it didn't make sense. If Kiedler was right that she was a corporate spy, wouldn't that make Chapek the issue after all?

I spent the rest of that night trying to find out more about her, Googling this and that, getting lost in the infinite labyrinth. I started with Carbon Audit. The home page was Reddit-like, an undifferentiated list of accumulated atrocities, as if the smallest violation were as evil as the largest. Chapek was only mentioned in one post that I could find, but Xcelsion was heavily referenced, though not as often as ExxonMobil, BP, or a Chinese company I'd never heard of before. One post compared Xcelsion at Rui Nodo to the Exxon Valdez in Alaska and Union Carbide in Bhopal. The comments below were predictably hostile and militant. Another post led to a GIF of a crude drawing of a slithering lizard that looked like a cross between an iguana and a salamander, labelled the *sphenomorphus* water skink or sea monkey, with a tag that read "65 million years of existence ended in one day." I found the drill-tracking site that Kiedler had mentioned, and saw a mix of blue and red dots all over the world. The South Pacific was not particularly dense with that measles-like rash, but there were drill platforms in

parts of the ocean I would never have imagined. In a way, it was fascinating to watch.

I left and visited the Chapek Energy home page, but other than typical investor relations material, there was not much to find, not even a company directory. As far as I could tell, the business had been launched fifteen years earlier, and did most of its work in offshore drilling. The CEO was named Peter Stoddard. I Googled him and discovered some interesting details. He was an old industry hand who'd gone maverick, a throw-back to boom/bust wildcatters like Getty and Hunt decades earlier. He looked like an asshole. Older but fit. A buzzed haircut. A razor-sharp line to his suit pants and cuffs. A severe but amused smile, as if he were about to make money off you or beat the shit out of you or both. I went for a more complete bio and found one on the Forbes website. A West Point grad. An MIT engineering degree. A few years with Midwest Hasting before going overseas for Shell and Amoco. Back with Midwest Hastings. Out again. Then a series of small drillers that got investment capital, used it up, went under, reformed with a different name. Finally, one of those names, Chapek Energy, seemed to stick.

I thought about that personal history, and tried to figure out why it bothered me. It wasn't just that Stoddard had done two stints with Xcelsion when it was still Midwest Hastings. Lots of oil guys had. There was something else. Then I remembered. West Point. Moss had gone there, too. I looked at the dates and saw that they had been classmates. They'd

graduated the same year. They'd known each other before their careers had even begun. I did not know how that factored in but it seemed significant.

And that led me to another strange thought. If Moss and Stoddard were the same age, was there anything between Stoddard and Amanda? I had picked up a few Google tricks in a short time, the primary one being that you could associate search terms together and thereby triangulate to some point of potential connection fairly easily. I Googled their names, expecting nothing special, but nine pages in I came up with a photograph. A deal-signing ceremony in Indonesia. I could not read the language of the newspaper article, but I could see names of foreigners written in English. Peter Stoddard and Amanda Barden. Could that be my Amanda? Standing in the crowd on the platform, it was easy to spot Stoddard. He was tall and dominating, broader shouldered than anyone around him, and wearing a bigger, meaner grin. Three places to Stoddard's right, the only white woman on the stage, but it was impossible to make her out. She was blurred by the scanning of the image that was scratched somehow directly across the face, as if some violence had been done to the original newspaper.

I poured myself a drink and sat on the balcony to think. An hour later I got a text from Kiedler.

"Don't do any searches on her. They'll know if you do, and they'll know it's us doing it."

Was Kiedler always monitoring my Internet use? *Fuck you*, I thought, and turned the phone off for the first time since I'd flown to the west coast.

An act of rebellion or surrender that tasted like scotch.

A few nights later, I could not stop myself from searching her again. In a place where there had been no information about her previously, I now found a photo and bio. She was the vice president of resource development at Chapek Energy. I had not expected her to be so senior. The photograph was a headshot. Her face was attractive in a suburban or southern kind of way. Eyes wide and eager, a nice, perhaps overly enthusiastic smile, blonde or dyed blonde hair, blown out, a quieter pink lipstick, a trace of eye shadow, expensive-looking earrings. She took care with her appearance but her expression seemed forced. She tried hard. Maybe in everything she did. I suspected she was from a modest background, and her education reinforced that impression. Her first three years of college had been spent at a school I'd never heard of, a community college in Texas, then there was a six-year gap before she attended Harvard where she got double masters in business and international relations. She must have done something right, been as bright as they get, otherwise Harvard would have been an impossible reach. She'd worked at Goldman for two years, Credit Suisse for three, then Xcelsion, where she oversaw a derivatives group. This floored me. She was a former Xcelsion employee.

We'd even overlapped by a year. I wondered if I'd handled her file at some point. Given her gender and Harvard background, and her fast

rise through technical functions and our diversity goals for women leaders, it surprised me that I didn't remember her, even with 40,000 employees. There was a huge need, a hunger, really, for female executives with high potential. I would have jumped on Amanda Barden if I'd known anything about her. I suppose, in my last year, I'd been distracted by my own downward spiral. Her employment with Chapek had started two weeks after her departure from Xcelsion. Nothing suspicious in that. In fact, it was a sign that she hadn't been caught up in any of the kickback stuff. She'd left of her own accord, a few months before the scandal first surfaced. A lucky move. She'd gotten out before Xcelsion began to bleed talent. The new firm was smaller but that was shrewd of her. Many women rose through the ranks faster by stepping aside from a big company and accumulating real P&L and oversight experience in a more aggressive environment, either at a start-up or at a subsidiary with a freer hand. We used to program those kinds of development paths on purpose when we were clever enough to make it happen.

With her track record, the sky was the limit for her career. So what did that say about the affair? Would she have seen Moss as a catalyst, a chance to secure an even more significant job? It didn't feel right to me. It seemed more likely that a notorious affair would jeopardize everything she'd ever tried to achieve. Was she married? Was she a mother? I wanted to search her more widely, to find more personal details. But going even a little deeper made

me wary of Kiedler. I had a sense he kept a closer tab on my online activities than any parole officer ever had.

The most difficult thing, in the ensuing weeks, was to continue working with Neville Moss. It wasn't that I particularly disliked the man, or found the time I spent with him so awful, it was the strain of leading a double life. I felt pulled in two directions at once, perhaps more than two. I was used to pretending. I was used to faking. But the stakes had never been so high, the attention so glaring. I felt like a political candidate on the campaign trail, never unguarded, never off-duty. I had to listen intently to Moss's life and opinions, to be held rapt by every word, and in the quiet moments, when I would have preferred to retreat into the sanctuary of my own aimless thoughts, I had to work instead to come up with astute questions, properly timed, calibrated to the mood and temper of the great man. I had to prompt Moss with leading observations. I had to invent details I wanted to know more about. All for the memoir I was never going to write.

Kiedler was travelling and couldn't meet in person but we debriefed on the phone every evening. I wanted to tell him what I had learned about Amanda, but there was no way I could do that without revealing that I'd done more searches. I took a different tack, and asked about Moss's wife.

"Becka?" Kiedler asked. "She's great. Honestly, I feel worse for her than anyone if this ever gets out. It actually makes me angry at Neville. What a mess."

"She's a lot younger than he is?" I asked, fishing.

"At least twenty-five years," Kiedler said.

It wasn't a surprise; in fact it confirmed what I expected. When it comes to top executives, second wives are usually roughly two decades younger. With third wives, it's fifty-fifty. They're either the same generation, or they drop another decade or even two. In other words, you either go back to having a companion or you double down and date your granddaughter's roommate. But Moss's choice in a mistress was a different story.

"Is Becka attractive?" I asked. I did not want to get too forward.

"I'll say. Why do you ask?" Not confrontational just curious, as though he respected my scientific method.

"I'm just wondering what kind of person Neville is drawn to." I felt the ice beneath me cracking, and tried to speed up. "I mean, is he attracted to someone he shares interests with, is it purely physical, does he want someone who looks up to him? I have so little to go on with Amanda." It was a mistake saying her name. To Kiedler, she was always 'her.' "How did Neville meet Becka?"

I expected a benefit party, a friend of a friend. But Kiedler's voice was colder, as though I had touched a nerve.

"Becka was one of Neville's temporary secretaries when Nancy was getting cancer treatment," Kiedler said. "We only knew the affair was going on after he made HR hire Becka as head of special events and entertainment. It got a bit messy. A minority

candidate had already been offered the job and the idiot at HR didn't have the balls to tell Neville. We paid out on that one. The board was going to issue a formal reprimand until Neville took matters out of their hands."

"How?" I asked, wondering about the machinations of the powerful.

"He divorced his wife and got engaged to Becka. Her final act as director of special events was organizing her own bridal shower."

"I see," I said. I felt misled, not lied to exactly, but all of the innocence and surprise about Moss's affair with Amanda seemed suddenly overblown. Who was kidding who? This was part of a pattern, not an outlier event.

"Weren't you worried he'd do something like that again?" I asked, a little more pointedly than I'd been so far.

"One of Nancy's performance criteria," Kiedler said, "is making sure something like that doesn't happen again, at least not office related."

I thought of Moss's efficient secretary, one of the coldest and most forbidding women I'd ever encountered.

"Right."

"We're not complete idiots," Kiedler said. "Most of the time."

They talk about Stockholm Syndrome, and how captives fall in love with their captors. Even as I recognized the elements of my own stalking syndrome, I could not help but feel deeply connected to Amanda

through the tenuous links of our correspondence. It did not matter whether she was part of some nefarious plot to undermine Neville Moss and Xcelsion. It did not matter whether she was a victim in her own right and the innocent object of Moss's obsession. Either way, I could surround her in narrative that made me want to know her more, to care for her even, to be part of her life. I could even hold multiple narratives in mind at the same time. If she was as daring and conspiratorial as Kiedler suspected, then she was my kind of daring and conspiratorial. There was a secret part of me that wanted to see Xcelsion and the entire apparatus of corporate America destroyed. If she was as innocent as the apparent facts would lead me to suppose, then I wanted to watch out for her, to warn her, to divert the coming shit storm. If she was somehow both those things at the same time then that was better still, my innocent conspirator, my anarchist naïf. Above all, I was lonely, I suppose. You would think that through my time in prison and at the call centre in Wisconsin, I would have grown accustomed to loneliness. But this was the loneliness of letting the world back in again. Perhaps because I was in nearly constant contact with Kiedler and Amanda by email and text, and in the company of Moss for many hours each day, I was achingly empty. It seemed to me that this mood, this malaise, this neediness began to seep into my emails to Amanda. Little by little, they became my only outlet for warmth and comfort.

"Thinking of you. Thinking of you. Thinking of

you," I wrote to her one night in a surge of ridiculous feeling, just before closing my eyes and trying to sleep. The king-size hotel bed was so large I left my laptop, files, phone, a few books, and a newspaper on one side, like it was a spare table.

An hour later, my phone lit up. I'd set it to illuminate and buzz whenever an incoming email or text arrived. I picked it up, so warm in my hand that it felt a part of me, indistinguishable from my own flesh, though I knew the heat came from the battery.

I was Pavlov's dog. The arrival of each new message filled me with the most peculiar mix of dread, anticipation, and sense of worth. I squinted against the glare, finding it difficult to focus for a moment, and saw finally that it was from her. Of course. Who else?

"I know you're not Neville Moss," she wrote.

I did not know what to say or think. I did not move for seconds, and then I wrenched and twisted until I was sitting up in bed. I sensed that I was not alone in the room. I turned on the light. I looked around. I put my hands to my head.

I wanted to talk to Kiedler immediately, but stopped myself. I didn't know what to do. My brain turned quickly to wild plans, running through a hundred different ways I could respond. I had a feeling, a strange, heart-thumping feeling, that a great deal was at stake, beyond this ridiculous covert business, beyond Neville Moss and Kevin Kiedler, beyond Xcelsion. Something fragile and precious inside me might die if I lied. Which was worse?

I wrote back with a simple question mark. I could summon no better subterfuge, no more subtle answer, no plausible rescue from the trouble I'd suddenly found myself in.

Her reply came shortly.

"So what do we do now?" she asked.

I don't know, I thought.

"I don't know," I wrote.

That Friday, Neville announced that he was going to spend the weekend at his house in Pescadero. I felt a surge of relief and exhaustion. I could use a day or two away from Moss, but Moss was not done with me.

"You can stay over," Moss said. "We'll put you in the carriage house so Becka's not put out. I don't think Debra's there this weekend."

"That would be great," I said, as agreeably and energetically as I could manage. Who was Debra? A daughter, a maid, a friend of the family?

Moss needed an hour. I wondered if I should run back to the hotel for a change of clothes. I texted Kiedler but Kiedler didn't answer. Foolishly, I asked Nancy who peered at me across the room with indifference and disdain.

"I have no idea," she said, unhelpful and disapproving at the same time.

So I did not go back to the hotel and did not leave the outer office. And when one hour went by and then another hour, I felt foolish, but I also felt relieved by the reprieve from Moss's attention and the mental demands of playing my role. Then Moss burst out of the room, his jacket on, wearing

sunglasses despite the darkness of the interior, and told Nancy he was on his way to Pescadero.

"Have a terrific weekend, Mr. Moss."

"You, too, Nancy. Don't do anything crazy now." And then to me: "Where's your bag? Never mind. There's stuff at the house. Let's get on the road before everyone else does."

The car was waiting outside. A black Mercedes Benz Maybach that looked subdued and compact on the outside, but was expansive and luxurious within. Three football players could have sat in the back.

Moss settled. "Let's make good use of this time," he said, and then said nothing. It was up to me to begin our conversation, to extract the precious elixir.

I struggled to straighten up and pull my notepad and pen from my bag. The effort cost me. Without realizing I had started, I heard myself asking questions.

"I'm thinking we should get your story down. Your life story. Not in any milestones kind of way, but what you went through in the early part of your career, what it was like."

"Shit," Moss said, and I wondered, wearily, if I'd taken the wrong tack.

"I don't reflect on it much," Moss continued. "I probably should. I'm sixty-four. I don't know how many years I have left."

"You seem healthy to me, sir."

"Well, that proves you're not a doctor. Let's see. I suppose my first job at Midwest Hastings is as good a place as any to start."

I nodded, pen poised. I should have interrupted. I should have asked Moss to go back farther, to talk about West Point, and the Groves Corporation, what it was like to develop energy policy at the Pentagon, not some staid gas company. But I didn't have it in me. I accepted the flow once I'd turned on the tap.

"At the time," Moss began, "Midwest was the largest gas company in the US, but gas was a sleepy industry then. Regulated to the hilt. Nothing there for an entrepreneur. But me and an old buddy, Pete Stoddard, shook things up. I started our trading desk. Pete was on the development side. Together we financed and built a dozen plants and a few lines. We saw how much America was growing. Any blind man could, but no one wanted to open their eyes to what was coming, the insatiable goddamn energy need. We pitched everyone on that problem, even competitors. People used to laugh at us, two guys just into their thirties, Pete and Moss. The joke was that in a million years we'd have to call ourselves crude and oil. Well, the joke was on them soon enough. Eric Waltz was getting ready to retire. If you ask me, he'd retired ten years before and had just forgotten to file. Used to be on the golf course by two every day. But he started grooming both of us for the top job. I'm not sure Pete even wanted it. He wasn't the big organization type. But I suppose it became a competitive thing because he wanted it bad enough by the end. I was a little more palatable to the board, always been good at politics, and I think my vision was a little stronger, hard-driving but not too out in front, conservative enough for those cowboys from Oklahoma. They gave it to me. I was thirty-two, and

one of the first things I had to do was fire Pete. It wasn't ego or revenge. He was financing projects in the goddamnedest way, shoving debt off the balance sheet and onto the next deal before it got accounted, using one book for internal and a second book as collateral, snowballing risk until it got bigger and bigger. He could have kept doing it, too, if he just took his foot off the gas a little, but Pete wasn't wired to back off. I guess that was the first hardest decision I ever had to make, firing a good friend. I'd like to say it doesn't get any easier, but it gets a lot easier. I wouldn't give it a second thought now. Put that in your book. Any CEO who says different is lying."

I was still surprised to hear him talking about the CEO of Chapek Energy, unbidden, and I didn't want him to stop.

"That's a great story," I said. "There's almost a mythic element to you and Stoddard, like Cain and Abel."

Moss laughed. "I'm glad you didn't say Bonnie and Clyde. Well, I don't think Cain would have hired Abel again, but I did. It wasn't an admission that I'd been wrong, it was just different timing, different needs. Once in a while you need someone like Pete Stoddard if you're running a big operation. He doesn't last long. You think I'm a hard-ass, you should see what that guy was like to work for. I remember one of his VPs, a big guy, ex-military, crying in my office because he couldn't take it. Pete obliterated obstacles. During the Triumph merger, we had a roomful of lawyers and Wall Street types working all night trying to hammer out the fine

print, and they were taking too long, according to Pete, and he tried to stay away and not go nuts, but he couldn't sleep so he drove back to the conference room at three in the morning and he screamed for everyone to line up against the wall, and when they were all standing there like they were about to be executed he said, 'Anyone who wants to get this deal done, stand still and don't move, and anyone who doesn't want to get it done, come forward because I am going to beat you to death right here and now and then I'm going to roll you up in this Oriental rug and personally carry you out to the fucking trash.' I think he meant it, too. Point is, they thought he meant it, and they got the deal signed within eight hours. Pete even docked the law firm nineteen thousand dollars for getting him out of bed, said his time was worth what they were billing for twenty-two lawyers.

"Anyway, that was around when I fired Pete again. Or he quit. Let's say he went away. Tended to his investments, from which he made quite a fortune. Probably worth ten times more than me today, and I took the straight and narrow. I kept building Midwest Hastings. I knew we needed to diversify out of gas. We were doing well, but regulations were killing us and even going international wasn't going to solve all our problems. Back then, you couldn't get a gas plant or refinery or pipeline built in the third world unless you owned the second son of whatever dictator was in power, and I didn't know how to play that game well enough yet, so we started buying small oil producers, ambitious outfits that needed capital to exploit their hunches. They were

drilling all over the world. Off the coast of Africa, in the jungles of Brazil, on islands in Indonesia you've never even heard of. You want a book? You should write about acquiring those wildcatters. They like your money just fine, but they don't even consider themselves under your authority until you get fed up and take the keys away. But every one of those guys is still a friend. Especially the guys I had to wrestle hardest. Now they all love me because I made them rich. It got easier as we got bigger. I didn't have to fly across the Pacific in the middle of the night and show up in some shit office with ex-military security. We became establishment, but I'd like to think we've never lost our drive for growth at all costs, our willingness to roll the dice on big opportunities. I may be losing my edge, but I'm still sharper and deadlier than most of the knives in the drawer, I bet."

"Is Pete Stoddard still one of those friends?" I asked. I got a curious look from Moss.

Moss laughed, but it was bitter rather than warm. "No, he's not. Stop here."

I stopped. Moss was not talking to me, however. The driver, who had seemed oblivious to the conversation, immediately pulled the car across the road and into a mall parking lot.

"I told Becka I'd pick up her favourite sherbet. Why don't you scribble until I'm back?"

Moss flung open the door, got out, and strode along the sidewalk. It was the kind of strip mall I had only seen in California, no connecting hallway inside, everything lined up outside like shops on an old main street.

I looked up and into the rearview mirror to check the driver and commiserate. He did not look back. I folded my notebook over my hand and closed my eyes.

My phone buzzed and lit up. I started, feeling a little sweaty from sleep, and fumbled until the phone was in my hand and turned around the right way. The number was Kiedler's. I answered.

"Where are you?" Kiedler asked. He sounded tired.

I struggled to remember.

"I'm with Moss."

"I know you're with Moss. I asked where are you?"

I looked around. "Some strip mall parking lot." I realized how vague that sounded. "We're on the way to the house in Pescadero."

"Is Neville there?"

"We stopped. He's getting something."

"Becka's sherbet."

I nodded, wearily. Why did Kiedler know that?

"We've been talking about Pete Stoddard," I said.

"Who?"

I knew then that Kiedler wasn't telling me everything. It was in his voice.

"Pete Stoddard. Moss's oldest friend and most bitter enemy, apparently. You know anything about him?"

"Yeah, he's her boss."

I wasn't expecting Kiedler to open up. It threw me off.

"Her?"

"Her."

"Oh." Then. "You're kidding."

"Of course I'm not kidding. Stoddard runs Chapek. She works at Chapek."

"I thought Chapek was not the issue. And now you're telling me she works for Moss's arch enemy?"

"I didn't want you to focus on something that was outside your main area of concern."

It surprised me that Kiedler, the Kiedler I'd once known, was capable of playing head games with me, though I could understand his reasoning. Even so, it did permit me to sound irate.

"Jesus, don't you think that could have been helpful information?"

"I don't know. I'm flying blind here. I'm making it up as we go."

"I get it," I said. And I did. "So that's why you thought she was planted in Moss's way."

"Yes."

"You think Stoddard is trying to undermine Moss for old time's sake."

"Maybe. I don't know. Whatever it is, I want it stopped."

"I understand."

"Why are you talking to Neville about Stoddard?"

"Because I'm supposed to be writing his memoir. Moss wanted to talk about the early days, and the early days seem to revolve around Stoddard."

"Yeah, I guess they do. We should stop talking about this on the phone."

"Well, when are we supposed to talk? I haven't seen you in three weeks."

"There's a lot going on. You're doing great. You're

keeping this moving. We have a small problem, however."

"Yes?" I did not like small problems. Inevitably, they were actually large problems.

"You remember the Carbon Audit story about the rig in the South Pacific?"

"Of course."

"CNN is reporting that it's a hoax."

"What do you mean?"

"The drilling, the reports of an earthquake. It was all an elaborate hoax. None of it happened. CNN is admitting it had the wool pulled over its eyes. They look like total idiots. They were ready to do a special on that lizard."

"The video of the island?"

Kiedler laughed. "It's actually from some B movie in the '70s. A Bond rip-off starring Lee Marvin, Richard Harris, and Jill St. John."

"So what's the problem?"

"The problem is that Carbon Audit has released a statement that they developed the hoax as a way of drawing attention to a secret drilling deal between Chapek Energy and Xcelsion."

"But there is no secret deal."

"Correct. But they're claiming they have evidence of email correspondence and secret meetings occurring at the highest levels."

"Holy shit, are they talking about Neville's emails?"

"Could be. Thank God we've laid the groundwork to undermine the credibility of those emails. But it's more crucial than ever that we get ahead on this. We have to tie up every possible loose end."

"I think I can arrange to see her," I said. The words were out before I could stop them.

"What do you mean?"

"I think I could arrange to meet her. Arrange for Moss to meet her, I mean. Somewhere neutral. A place Moss might go on business. Then I could confront her with what we know, figure out what I can, scare her off."

Kiedler didn't speak. I waited. I remembered to breathe.

"That's not a bad idea," Kiedler said.

"That's what I'm thinking." I didn't know what I was thinking.

"It would accelerate everything."

"It's probably now or never," I said.

"I suppose you're right," Kiedler said. "Let me think."

"Moss is coming. I see him walking toward the car."

"Fine. Do it. Make the arrangement. See if you can swing her. Subtle. Softly, softly, catchee monkey."

"What?"

"Something my mother used to say."

The door opened, I hung up.

"Did you get it?" I asked. It seemed a ridiculous question.

"Who were you talking to?" So Moss had noticed.

"Kiedler. We needed to catch up."

"Alright, let's get going. I don't want to keep Becka waiting."

"I can't," I said.

"What?" It was possible no one had said that to Neville Moss before.

I quit, I wanted to say. Instead: "Kiedler needs me to come back."

I opened the door and stood on the curb.

"Don't worry about me, I'll get a taxi back."

If Neville Moss was worried about me, he did not show it as the Maybach left the parking lot.

In the taxi, during the long ride home, I texted her.

"I need to see you," I said.

"Yes," she answered. And then. "I'm scared."

3

I flew to New York but not directly. My connections took me first to San Francisco, then to Dallas where I caught the last flight of the evening to La Guardia. I wore a sports coat and slacks and looked like every other business traveller, another soldier in the great corporate army, crammed into coach with carry-on bags stuffed overhead like multimodal shipping containers, biding time until the cell phones could be turned back on. I tried to close my eyes and calm down. She sat five rows up, and on the aisle seat across. I tried not to glance over too often.

It was a terrible flight. Twice, the plane dropped so suddenly that I braced myself with one hand on the armrest and one hand on the seat before me, wondering when the plummet would stop or whether the wings might snap off the fuselage. The head flight attendant announced on the intercom that meals couldn't be served because of the turbulence, though the smell of over-heated food filled the cabin and the curtains to business were closed. The flight attendants bobbed and weaved their way down the aisle offering mini-packs of pretzels and drinks of

water, joking about the inconvenience. The descent was even worse. With the lights of Manhattan in view, the plane swayed from side to side like a child's toy, before the tires finally smacked. Wet on the windows, wet on tarmac. The captain came on the radio immediately, something I didn't recall ever happening during other flying experiences, sounding proud of pulling off the landing, as though he'd already pounded back a couple to celebrate.

"Congratulations, folks. We're the last flight in tonight. They're shutting down the runways after us."

I saw a few passengers smile in relief, heard a few groan.

The head flight attendant broke in, officious and harried, apologizing to passengers with connecting flights, offering the services of the information officers at the gate to assist, reiterating the necessity of staying seated, insisting that there was no urgency, all would be taken care of. People around me got busy, powering up cell phones, checking emails and v-mails, following threads, furthering loops. Amanda, I noticed, didn't bother.

The plane neared the gate. At the chime, everyone sprang upward like one multi-headed beast, grappling with overhead suitcases, stepping into the aisle, pushing forward whenever possible, jostling for progress. I tried to appear indifferent but forward-directed. Like everyone else, including her, my pace and stride length increased as the walkway opened wider and I shot into the terminal.

I had no choice but to go to the restroom. For

hours, the flight had been too rocky to get out of my seat. I tried not to let the diversion make me anxious but it did. Never had standing in front of a urinal taken so long.

I power-walked out of the terminal, hoping to see her somewhere near the baggage carousel. She was nowhere in sight. Maybe she'd made a direct run for a cab. I stepped outside to check. The taxi queue was endless. It stretched beyond the concrete awning and into the open air where a resigned few stood beneath the lashing rain, all the more pathetic for the indifference they showed.

I contemplated entering the downpour, and realized I'd already lost.

A Middle Eastern man wearing a suit and tie approached and asked in a low voice if I wanted a taxi. I said yes. It seemed the only answer. Jump in a limo at whatever cost and race into Manhattan to the hotel, hope that I could find her quickly. Then I saw her walking toward the exit, just passing the carrousel, and realized she must have stopped at a restroom, too. I breathed again, and tried to relax the flinch in my expression.

I recognized her face. She wore a skirt suit and heels, carried a purse, pulled her small suitcase by a handle. She looked composed and dignified, a determined stride, a classy bearing, not at all self-conscious, her head up, her gaze forward. She was tall, maybe close to six feet, a bit broad in her shoulders and thick in her calves. The limo driver was watching her, too, and I handed him a twenty so that he would understand it was important.

"Tell that woman her limo is waiting and bring her back here."

The man did not hesitate, even if my request struck him as strange and perhaps improper. Amanda stopped as the driver reached her, though her body leaned slightly toward the exit. I saw her glance my way, and look back to the driver immediately. Then I saw her nod.

As they approached, the limo driver could not resist the line of a smile, as though he'd arranged an assignation.

I was impressed by how calm she looked. When she saw me, her composure changed, ever so slightly, revealing anxiety beneath.

You? her eyes said.

I nodded to acknowledge the unlikely truth.

We walked with bent heads through the rain into the parking lot.

We were silent in the car for the first five minutes. The confined and humid space smelled of wet clothes, wet mats. The driver did not make small talk. Her stockinged legs were pressed primly together and angled to the side to make room for her height. She did not flinch or fidget, but stared directly ahead, as if watching for a destination she'd never visited before. Only her hands seemed out of place. They lay on her lap as though detached, the only part of her that communicated any helplessness. In contrast, I was relaxed on the outside but in turmoil within. I took nonchalant glances out the window, at the driver, at her knees, and wondered if I would fuck up.

Finally, as the car entered the relentless flow of traffic heading for Manhattan, she glanced at me, cleared her throat, and spoke in a muted voice.

"How does it start?"

"We talk," I answered.

A flinch around her mouth.

"About what?"

"The truth."

"The truth," she repeated.

I didn't know how to interpret her tone. Bitterness?

"The facts."

"Is this what I think it is?" she asked.

"We need to know everything," I said, sticking to Kiedler's script, wanting to change it. "Every detail. Everything that was said and done. How it started. How long it went on. Every contact you had with him. Even what you wanted to happen that didn't happen."

She shifted in her seat and folded her arms, still defiant.

"I bet you do," she said, like there was something vaguely perverse or gynecological about the probing.

I was surprised by her nerve. Women were tougher than men. Women at her level were tougher than men at any level.

"I should have known this wasn't going to be a date with my secret admirer. Who are you with?" she asked, and rattled off initials, pointedly: "SEC? DOE? FBI?"

"No, no," I said.

"Then you're with Xcelsion."

"Yes," I admitted, another thing Kiedler had told

me not to say. "I want to help you, though. I want this to be resolved and to go away. I need your help to make that happen."

She looked out the window. She must have felt trapped, lied to. I was contributing to that. In place of honesty, I had decided to play a role, at least temporarily. At some level, it was close to the truth.

"What about the emails and texts?" she said. "Those were you?"

"We started monitoring your communications with Moss. We began to reply to them."

"For how long?"

"About four months," I lied. Kiedler's lie.

"The whole time," she said. "Does Neville know?"

"Not about this," I said.

Showing cards I didn't need to show. I did it for her. To offset the humiliation.

"What does he know?"

"Nothing. He just knows it's over."

"Over," she said, scornful again.

"We need to know why."

Her quick turn of head, her angry glare. It was enough to convince me that it had never been as Kiedler feared. A set up. A conspiracy.

"Ask Neville why."

"We can't."

"Of course you can't. You need to protect the great man from any consequences."

"You know what I mean."

"I'm not sure I could ever know what someone like you means."

"I think you know it's not quite like that."

I could tell she didn't believe me. I stopped talking, and gave her the time and space to accept what was unfolding.

Kiedler had told me not to let her out of my sight, but that sort of watchfulness seemed ridiculous and unseemly now. While she checked in, I waited in the lobby, pretending to read emails from my phone, and checked in after she had disappeared in the elevator bank. There was some confusion. The room had been booked in Neville Moss's name, but I explained that Mr. Moss was not able to travel, and I had come in his place. I wondered how that particular screw-up had occurred. The desk clerk did an inordinate amount of typing on his console afterwards, and it occurred to me that my room was being downgraded accordingly. When I finally got there, I found a typical New York-size hotel room, meaning small, the view outside a massive air conditioning unit on the roof of the next building over.

I gave her another fifteen minutes to refresh, then put my jacket back on and walked the hallway to the elevator. She was three floors up. It was eleven o'clock. The hotel felt empty, but I knew there were lives behind each door, though few so complicated in that moment as hers or mine.

I knocked lightly. When she opened I saw that she had changed into jeans and a t-shirt and that her feet were bare. This made her seem younger and far less assertive, an ordinary woman on a business trip relaxing in her hotel room, watching HBO and

drinking a glass of wine. Was this intentional, a way of swaying the executioner? I decided that she didn't do intentions well. She was, for whatever reason, not very deft with her physical appearance. She didn't know how to use that aspect of herself. The properties of her body were inert to her, like her hands had been, laying on her lap in the taxi.

The room was larger than I expected, a suite. A separate bedroom, the door half open, a living room with couch, lounge chair, television, and desk. I felt overdressed. I wanted to comfort her but I had a job to do first, for her sake even more than mine.

I sat on the edge of the lounge chair and she sat on the couch.

"I ordered food," she said. "I figured you might want something."

"Thanks."

"A drink?"

"Sure."

She fished through the mini-bar for a couple whiskeys and a coke and tonged some ice into a water glass. A bit of the Southern Belle in the way she did that. The TV was on, a news channel, the sound muted, but impossible not to follow the coverage because of all the text on the screen. An earthquake in the Midwest.

"You're not what I expected," she said.

"How do you mean?" I asked. I did, and did not, want to know more.

"At first, in the car, I was expecting Romeo. And of course you're not Romeo. But you're not a fixer either. Or a lawyer. Or a security consultant. You

seem decent. Maybe even kind. Can you tell me your name?"

Kiedler had told me not to get personal, to offer as little of myself as possible, but of course that was impossible.

"Reid," I told her. "Reid Frank."

Why had I told her my old name? It was stupid and impossible to take back. I'd made my first foolish mistake, perhaps a fatal one.

"Thank you," she said. "I'm Amanda."

I already knew that, of course. Amanda Barden.

I should have said something, but I was wavering, losing my determination.

"Where were we?" she asked, as though she were helping me along.

"We're figuring out your story. If it doesn't fit, we'll invent a version that does."

"Oh, is that what we're doing. And why should I participate in your story-making?"

"Because if you don't, you will have no influence on the narrative that will play out." Glib, unnecessarily cool.

"Jesus." She looked back to the TV. "What narrative is that?"

"The conniving narrative. The embezzlement narrative. The career-climber-who-used-any-tool-available-to-her-to-get-what-she-wanted narrative. That's what they want to do, you realize. They've prepared the groundwork to catch you in a lie if this ever goes public. It will be you who is ruined, not Neville Moss."

They, not me. I wonder if she guessed.

She laughed. "Which story would you prefer?" She was far more relaxed and playful than I was, even in my position of advantage. At some level I was impressed, perhaps even in awe.

"We want the truth, then we'll shape it to serve everyone's needs. We want to look good. We want you to look good."

"I bet." She got up from the couch. "Time for another drink."

The food arrived. When she lifted the silver covers off the plates I saw that she'd ordered a club sandwich and fries for me, a single avocado for herself. It was neatly vivisected in the middle, the halves still pressed together, though slightly off-kilter, propped up by a sprig of parsley. I could not hide my surprise. That was dinner? When she opened the cover of the avocado there was a sucking sound, and a perfectly spherical half stone was revealed. She picked up the other half, with its negative imprint, and spooned out a dollop of the soft meat and brought it to her mouth like she was enjoying a touch of sorbet. She ate two more scoops, and had not even finished cleaning out the husk of the first side before she put the spoon next to the avocado and covered the plate. Evidently, dinner was just for me. I devoured the club in a shower of crumbs. I loaded salt on the fries. I would have spooned up the ketchup if I'd been alone.

"I like to see someone enjoy their food," she said. "It's still fascinating."

"Aren't you hungry?" I asked.

"I don't have a stomach," she said.

I tried to grasp her meaning. Stomach for what? For risk, love, notoriety? But not that. Something more.

"I don't understand," I said.

"You don't know?" she asked.

I wondered how much I didn't know.

"They want me to hear it from you," I answered, as indifferently as I could.

Her look of scorn. She didn't believe me.

"I had my stomach removed," she said. "Radical gastric bypass surgery. That's how I met Neville."

"At a hospital?" I wanted to know more about her stomach, to understand what she meant, but I needed to follow Neville.

"On the island."

"What island?"

"Rui Nodo."

My mouth opened, ever so slightly.

"Rui Nodo," I managed to say. "Where's that?"

"In the South Pacific," she said. "About a thousand miles from Tahiti."

I could not completely trust my ears, or my memory, but I knew where I had heard the name before.

"I don't understand," I said. "How could you meet on an island in the middle of the South Pacific?"

"There's an advanced medical resort there called Saffron Hills. It's run by the Raffles Health Group in Singapore. Exclusive clientele. Royalty. Movie stars. Billionaires. People who run companies."

"And you."

"And me. It was my bonus. I'd closed a deal for a gas plant in Indonesia. Arranged all the financing, overcome the local bureaucracy, bribed everyone who needed bribing, and the stress and my bad health had almost killed me. My boss wanted me to get well. I was always heavy, but I had become obese, it was ruining my life, and my career. The travel. The shitty meals. The terrible work schedules. My own issues. I didn't want to have surgery. But I told myself that if I ever reached three hundred pounds I would do it. Then, one morning, I was three hundred and two, and I broke down and wept because it terrified me so much. I didn't eat for the next twenty four hours, not so much as a crumb, and when I stepped on the scale the next morning I was three oh nine."

She took a sip of the whiskey in the glass.

"Those seven pounds," she said. "I couldn't figure out where the hell they'd come from. I felt like my weight was a cancer, multiplying cells."

"So you went there for your surgery."

"And stayed for the recovery."

"That must have cost a fortune."

She shrugged. "The company paid."

"What was Moss doing on the island?"

She looked at me curiously.

"His own surgery."

"He had his stomach removed, too?"

"He had his heart and lungs removed."

"I don't understand."

"Heart lung transplant. Neville Moss was a very sick man. Now he's better. It seemed almost routine. His recovery was half as long as mine."

I did not know what to say. It couldn't be true. Surely, Kiedler would have told me.

"How could that not be public knowledge? They'd need to disclose."

"They hid it. Maybe they didn't want to rock the share price while he was so ill. Maybe they didn't want to cede power to an interim CEO. I wasn't supposed to run into him, I know that much."

"Holy shit," I said.

Was that why Kiedler was so concerned about Amanda—because she knew? Had Carbon Audit developed a hoax about a rig that had sunk off the coast of Rui Nodo to bring attention to the meeting between a Chapek executive and Neville Moss? I saw, for the first time, a way out for her, a possible escape.

"Did you know it was Neville when you saw him?"

"I did. I mean, I wasn't sure for about ten minutes. He was in recovery. He'd been resurrected from the dead. But I recognized him. When he started walking around the grounds for the first time, he was very ill and thin. I didn't want to run into him so I stayed away. I actually left whenever he came near. I think that's what made him interested in me in the first place. He saw me as elusive. And then, one day, he cornered me, and made me sit with him. We talked for hours. And he said at the end he felt like I really knew him, in a way that he hadn't felt known in years. Of course I knew him. But I didn't realize that he didn't remember me."

"You'd met before?"

"We'd met a few times. Once at Xcelsion. Once

at an industry event where he was awarded energy producer of the year. And twice sitting across the table from Indonesian government officials. He just didn't recognize me. Or he hadn't noticed me before. Or he'd seen right through me. I think that's when I knew my surgery had been a good thing. I was transformed in someone's eyes. I had been a spectacle before, or an invisible person, and now I was a member of the human race again."

How much self-loathing that revealed.

"So your affair began on the island?"

I did not want to be so direct, but I needed to understand.

"I never considered it an affair," she said. "It was chaste. We never made love. We never even made out. I doubt he was physically capable because of the surgery. Probably still isn't. But he was not normal emotionally. I'm not saying he was unhinged. But every single thing had become emotionally intense for him. He was feeling very deeply because of the transplant. I've read that it can be like that. I had something taken out, something that made me more restrained, put me more in control of my urges, my compulsions. He had something put in, something that made him feel things, physiologically, emotionally, psychologically, that he wasn't used to feeling or needing. I suppose that's why he fell in love with me. I didn't understand it at first, and when I did, I told him everything about me. Who I was. That I worked for Chapek. That we'd met before. But by then it was too late. He had come to believe I was the one for him, and I was trapped."

"And you kept it a secret."

I was trying to build her case. I wanted to find the solution.

"I spent the next three weeks trying to deter him," she said. "But he was persistent. Intense. And I started to miss him when I hadn't heard from him. I'm divorced. I don't have children. I work all the time. Since I was sixteen years old, the longest I have gone without working was on that island. We weren't even allowed cell phones. No trading. No business calls. No news. Every luxury and resource of the facility at your disposal, all inclusive in a single fee, which I wasn't paying. And now I'm back. And look what life has brought me."

She stopped. I did not know what to say.

"But it wasn't him, these past few months, it was you."

"Yes," I said.

"So what does that mean?"

I knew what I wanted to say. That it meant something. But even though I felt that way, I was worried, more worried than ever, that something bad could happen. I needed to prevent that. To save the life she had built.

"Tell me what I need to know, Amanda."

She looked peeved, as if I had destroyed the mood. Used her.

"What exactly do you need to know?"

"Is there anything more? Is there anything they can use against you? Did he call you? Are there any recordings? Did he give you anything?"

I wondered if she would notice that I said "they."

"I've got no secret tapes. I've received no expensive jewellery. Whatever Neville has ever said

to me is in that pile of emails and texts you've so carefully managed. I've told you everything there is to tell about me and Neville."

"What about Peter Stoddard, your CEO?" Thinking like Kiedler. "They know each other. They had a falling out. Could Stoddard be using you?"

"I don't think Pete spends much time worrying about Neville at all. But I'm certainly not privileged to know his inner thoughts."

We were sitting very close together. I looked down at her hand, the hand that did not seem to belong to her.

"I need to make a call," I said.

Her hand went to her lap, as if she'd just noticed it.

"Of course you do."

"I want to keep talking but I need to make this call."

"Who's stopping you?"

The reception in my room was poor. I tried Kiedler's number three times and couldn't get through. Even the texts failed. I needed to use the bathroom desperately. I needed to change my socks. My feet were soaked. I needed to brush my teeth. I looked at my face in the mirror and didn't recognize the person staring back in the harsh light. Who have you become? I needed to talk to Kiedler. I decided to go down to the lobby and try again.

Empty, dim, bordered by giant wax-leafed plants, like a jungle clearing. At the desk, a bellhop looked over to me, then back down to his paperwork. I

stood near the piano and tried the number again.

Kiedler answered. He sounded weary.

"I'm sorry I'm late," I said.

"Where are you?"

"At the hotel. In the lobby."

"Did you connect with her?"

"I've spent the last hour with her getting the story."

"Alright, tell me."

I told him. The stomach operation. The island. Meeting the old man. The nature of the relationship. I wanted Kiedler to chime in, to acknowledge the transplant, and its cover-up, but Kiedler didn't bite.

I waited. I held my breath.

Kiedler sighed. "That's all?"

"There's no there there," I said.

"I suppose it was worth it to find that out. You're tired. I can tell. You've done good. Everything I've asked. Now go to bed. Get some rest. We'll talk tomorrow about next steps. I need to think this through with a clear head."

"Okay," I said. I hung on. "I'll talk to you tomorrow."

"Frank?"

I thought about hanging up. There was something admonishing in his voice, some concern that had woken. I didn't want to hear it.

"Yeah?" I asked.

"Don't go back to her room."

I played innocent.

"What do you mean?"

"It's over. Don't take it any further."

"Of course, I won't." The furthest thing from my mind.

"I'm serious."

"I get it. Don't worry."

"Okay."

I hung up and looked around, conscious suddenly that I'd been speaking loudly and insistently in a public place. A man and a woman behind the front desk, doing paperwork. A hotel guest crossing the lobby for the front doors. Had they heard anything? I walked toward the front desk and nodded at the bellhop as I went by. He looked strangely familiar. How long had it been since I'd stayed in an expensive hotel? I reached the elevator. It opened almost immediately. I stepped inside and pressed the button for her floor.

When she opened the door, it was as though our first meeting—the one in which I'd played corporate problem-solver—had been an elaborate role-playing game, and this second meeting was between our true selves, without guise or artifice. We stumbled into each other. We pulled off clothes as we tripped and tumbled our way to the bed. We made love fiercely and tenderly, with desperation and humour.

"I missed you," she said.

I wasn't sure if she meant that she'd missed me for the twenty minutes I'd been away or in some larger sense, as though we'd missed each other for our whole lives. Perhaps it wasn't one or the other. Perhaps, in the logic of dreams, it was both.

"Why do you do this work that you do?" she asked.

And I began to tell her. I told her that I'd worked for Xcelsion and that I'd been fired. That I'd gotten addicted to gambling and it had become impossible for me to stop, despite my promise to Meeks and myself to get everything under control, and that instead I'd set up dummy expense accounts for hundreds of employees who didn't exist, making up names and jobs and work histories, just to siphon their travel and training budgets into my own personal slush fund, a pyramid scheme that seemed to be working until it stopped. And that I'd gone to prison and that my wife had divorced me and taken our daughter away, and that I was unemployable in any normal way, and that Kiedler had needed me to help his CEO, Neville Moss, out of a jam.

"And I'm the jam," she said.

"I'm going to help you," I said. "I'm going to solve this."

I kissed her ear and touched her belly with my hand, tracing lines with my finger. She told me I wouldn't find a scar.

"I understand your need to fill the emptiness," she said. "For me, it was food. Removing my stomach was the only way I could gain control over my life."

"How do you survive?" I asked. "Without a stomach."

"Very deliberately," she said. "Very carefully. Small portions. Supplements. Power shakes. The most difficult part is mental. But I know that if I was ever to gorge myself again I'd burst open inside. I'd die writhing in agony."

I held her more tightly than before and brushed the hair from her face.

"It's okay," she said. "He says that our whole society is addicted. That we consume too much. That we need a new relationship to capitalism, and that it starts with energy. He thinks we should all get our stomachs removed. That alternative energy means freedom from old addictions. He's actually funding secret research into the economic and wellness benefits that would accrue from gastric bypass surgery on a societal scale."

"Neville Moss?" I said.

"Peter Stoddard," she said, "the CEO of Chapek. You should come work for us. It's like no company you've ever encountered. It's rational and open. It's caring and nurturing. It's dedicated to higher values like sustainability and the ethical exploitation of resources. Peter wants us to become enriched as individuals and as a society through the work we do together. From each according to his ability, to each problem according to its needs. You'd feel at home with us. Your life would be transformed."

"I'd like that," I said. I did not believe it. Deep in that place where I believed nothing. But I wanted to believe it. And I wanted to keep all doubts and questions from her, forevermore.

"What about Neville?" I said. I meant, what are we going to do about him? How do we stop him from destroying Amanda's life? How do we keep the whims and appetites of such a monster from destroying the world? He was insatiable.

She laughed and stretched out to the night table beside the bed and showed me a paperback book.

"You asked me before if he'd ever given me

anything, and I forgot about this. His big extravagant present." I saw a lewd, garish cover, a jungle opening onto a beach, a man wearing a grey suit and a fedora with a pistol, holding hands with a beautiful and buxom woman in a red bikini. *Attack of the Sea Monkeys*. She opened it up.

"'I yearn for you, Amanda. I am your knight in grey-suited armour. Nev.' How can I hate him? He's just a boy at heart. Peter will convince him there's a better way."

Yearn, I thought. The kind of word I would have put in one of Neville's emails just to give him that awkward, endearing touch.

I woke up. Drunk. Hungover. Numb. Lying beside her. I needed to use the bathroom. It was pitch black. I groped, feeling for the night table. My hand found what I was looking for, the paperback. It was the only physical evidence that they'd ever been together. I clenched it. I stumbled out of bed. The room was huge. I didn't know where I was going. I sought the bathroom to relieve myself, to look at the book in private. I found the door, opened it, and stepped inside. The door, surprisingly heavy, swung shut behind me. The velocity of it. The decisiveness of the click was my nightmare. I turned and pushed and couldn't open it.

I was naked and outside in the hallway. I knocked discretely at first, afraid to make a commotion. When there was still no response, I began pounding on the door, hissing her name. I heard a door slam from within one of the nearby rooms. A cluck of

disapproval. Someone didn't like the fuss I was making.

"Amanda!" I called.

Amanda didn't answer.

"Amanda," I said.

I leaned my forehead against the door and didn't know whether to laugh or cry.

Final, inconvertible proof I'd been a fuck-up my entire life.

What would my wife say to that?

I thought of the bellhop, the strange familiarity of his face. I thought of the empty atrium. Its dim light. If I could make my way to the fringe of palm trees. Hide behind one, like Adam cast out of Eden, and call out in a hushed voice. Maybe then, the humiliation would be milder. Bellhops were accustomed to handling various embarrassments. Overflowed toilets. Handcuffs that wouldn't unlock. Heart attacks. Jealous spouses. Discretion was required by the job.

The prospect of the elevator terrified me. What if it stopped on its way down? I would be unable to keep the doors from opening wide, exposing me fully to the person standing outside. I looked for stairs. Absurdly, in my hand, I still clenched Moss's paperback, which I held instinctively in front of my genitals. I ran, as lightly as possible, down the long hallway, paused to peer around the corner, and saw a red exit sign. Losing composure. Feet pounding. Reached the door. Escaped into the brightness of a concrete and gun-metal stairwell, the echo of the door an explosion.

I leaned against the wall. Cold. Relieved. Shaking. I could have laughed but my shame was too overpowering. This was me all along. I'd ignored Kiedler and gone back to her because, after all, who would know? Now I was going to end up in the tabloids or on some gossip website trading in public humiliation. The surface of the stairs was sharp with thousands of puckered edges. I could barely step without wincing painfully. I twisted my gait to turn my feet sideways and avoid as much of the tread as possible. I made my way down those thirty-eight flights of stairs like I was descending a treacherous mountain.

My feet bleeding before the halfway mark. Smears of red in the harsh light, bloody prints. My teeth chattering uncontrollably. Groans coming from my throat.

Had the whole night gone by when I finally pushed open the door and saw the lobby?

It was, as I suspected, utterly quiet, the lights slightly dim, but I felt the warmth within like the rising of the sun after a long, chilled night. The softness of tile and then carpet under my feet. I approached the open area cautiously, slowly, though I wanted to run forward like the survivor of a shipwreck greeting his rescue. I stopped behind a palm tree and peered between the leaves.

I allowed my eyes to adjust to the dimness. I allowed my ears to still the tinny echoes that still sounded in my head.

I had, I realized, an overpowering need to relieve myself. That's why I'd woken in the first place, and yet my bladder had contracted with my fear and it

was only now that the urgency returned. There was no place to go. No restroom nearby. Standing behind the plant, already naked, I did what was easiest. My urine drilled holes in the dirt and drove the smell of wet, pungent earth into the air around me.

Finished, feeling that much better, more relaxed even, I edged my way along the wall to the corner and peered with a better sight line toward the front desk. I saw the bellhop. So far away. I hissed. The bellhop didn't look up. I called out, "Excuse me!" The bellhop looked up, but did not know where the sound had come from. I stepped forward and then stopped. The glass doors of the hotel entrance slid open, voices, laughter, a group of men and women. They were young, they were drunk, they were rich. A dozen or more, stumbling, falling into one another. One of them, a man, called out to the bellhop and staggered toward him, asking whether room service was still available. I saw the bellhop brace himself with a thin smile, and heard him respond that the kitchen was open twenty-four hours a day. The rest of the pack headed toward the elevator bank where I was hiding.

It was over. I was trapped. I leaned against the wall, accepting its support. It was difficult to refrain from sliding to the floor in a shameful huddle. Then I saw the fire alarm.

I was not the only guest who needed a bathrobe. I saw three others, as naked as I was, or nearly so. A young couple, huddled into each other, laughing, and one older man, heavy, balding, wearing dress shoes but no socks, with a white hand towel pressed into his groin. The blaring siren, heavier and slower than I would have expected, drove them all out into the street. I huddled in the plushness of the robe, grateful for it, and did not even mind standing on the wet pavement in my cut feet. My real misery was over. The rain had stopped. There were hundreds of people outside waiting, the atmosphere of delayed emergency, the bright lights and sirens. Firemen entered. Floors, reportedly, were being searched. I looked for Amanda but could not find her in the crowd.

The siren stopped, a sudden ending. Fifteen minutes later, we were allowed to shuffle back into the lobby, overflowing it. Many had forgotten their pass keys, and were asked to be patient. My plan, spontaneously arrived at, proved to be ingenious. I was finally brought, as the sky lightened outside, from the atrium into the elevator and up to the

thirty-fifth floor with a group of a dozen others.

"Is this your room, sir?" the young man asked.

I nodded. "It is."

The pass key opened the door.

"Are you sure?"

"I'm sure. Thank you. I'll get you a tip."

"That's not necessary. I hope you can get some sleep."

I stepped inside.

"Sir? Your feet. Are they cut?"

I closed the door.

I filled the bath with the hottest water it could produce and sat in it, a wet cloth on my head. I wished the lights were off but had no will or strength to rise and reach them. I fell asleep in the water and woke up because it had cooled. My feet were mauled, like tenderized meat. It was difficult to stand. I made my way to the bed and crawled into the sheets, still pressed flat, unused. I should call her, I thought. I needed to explain. She would be angry at me, hurt, or worried. I did not have my cell phone. I roused myself to lift the room phone and dial the hotel operator. I would tell her what happened. I would laugh with her, the anonymous alarm puller. It rang six times before she picked it up.

"Hello?"

A man's voice.

I hung up. They must have connected me to the wrong room. When I tried again, the operator did not answer.

I awoke. My room was still dark. Or had it darkened again? I didn't understand. There was a pounding noise and voices calling out. For a moment, I thought I had dreamed it all. That in my dream I was still running down a hallway. Naked. Locked out. Fearfully creeping stairwells, hiding behind plants, pulling alarms. Then I realized that the pounding and the voices were at my door. I got out of bed and stood, wincing and off-balance, remembering the soreness of my feet. I stumbled into a pair of jeans and an undershirt and made my way clumsily toward the door, asking who was there.

"Hotel security."

I sagged at the awareness that I hadn't escaped after all.

"What's wrong?"

"We need to speak with you, sir."

I opened the door. The bellhop and two men in suits. One tall, gaunt and bald, the other heavy, his chest and shoulders stretching his jacket wide, a walrus moustache, a ziplock baggy pinched between fingers.

"Is this your phone and wallet, sir?"

I stared. I'd forgotten that I'd left them in Amanda's room. My clothes, too. My passkey.

"Yes," I said, and tried to think quickly. Amanda had probably checked out. She might have turned my things into the front desk or left them in the room for housekeeping to find. Angry at me. Mystified. Embarrassed. "I've been looking for them." And then, my brain racing ahead. "I wonder if I dropped them in the lobby or in the stairwell during the fire alarm. Did somebody turn them in?"

"Nobody turned them in, sir. Would you come with us?"

"What do you mean?"

"We have some questions we need to ask you."

"What sort of questions?"

They told me they would rather clear the matter up without calling the police, but that was up to me.

A small office, a closed door, three chairs in the confined space. Two chairs against one. The gaunt guard, whose name was Leon, remained standing. The heavy guard with the moustache, whose name was Ron, sat in front of me, so close that our knees were almost touching.

"We take incidents in this hotel very seriously," Ron said.

"I understand," I said.

Should I admit the fire alarm?

"You're not Neville Moss," Ron began.

I was surprised until I remembered the confusion when I'd registered.

"No," I said. "I work for his company. The registration was under his name."

"Neville Moss was never here?" Ron pressed.

"Not to my knowledge," I said carefully. Absurdly, I thought of the male voice that answered when I called her room. Had that been Moss?

"The guest in room 3816," Leon said, his first words.

"Room 3816," I repeated, as though puzzled.

"Where we found your belongings. What was your relationship?"

I looked at the dull, paint-flaked walls, so at odds with the luxury of the hotel. How could I possibly explain my relationship with Amanda?

"We didn't have one," I said, "until tonight." I could not bring myself to say more.

Leon stared from above.

"Tell us," Ron said, "how you met."

"We shared a car into the city from the airport," I said.

"Why?" Leon asked.

"It was raining and there weren't many cabs and limos. We'd been on the same flight. We happened to be going to the same hotel."

"I love the happened part," Leon said to Ron.

"How did you end up in her room?"

"Yes," Leon said. "What else happened to happen?"

I was tired already of the good-cop bad-cop routine. I looked back to Ron.

"She asked me to come to her room to have a bite to eat."

"I think I'm going to throw up," Leon said.

"We had some room service. We talked for a while. Then I went back to my room and made a phone call for work."

"Isn't that late for a work call?"

"The call was to the west coast. So it was only around nine or so there."

A point for me.

"According to our records, your pass card was used to open your room door, room 3536, at 11:38 P.M. Then it is not used again. And yet the pass card

was found in room 3816 this morning. How did it get from your room to her room?"

"Is she okay? What's going on?"

"How did your pass card get into her room?" Leon asked.

I tried to gather the loose threads of my many thoughts.

"I couldn't make the call in my room because the reception was so bad," I heard myself saying. "So I went down to the lobby."

Ron looked up at Leon.

"West side, above twenty eight," Leon said. "AT&T dead zone."

"You made your call in the lobby. Then what? You didn't go back to your room. Where did you go?"

I didn't answer. Suddenly, Leon clapped his hands together in front of my face.

"Wake up," he said.

"I went back to her room."

"Now we're getting somewhere."

"And?" Ron said.

"That's private."

"Well then, you can share your secrets with the police."

"What do you mean?"

"At four this morning, you ordered more room service to her room."

"You must have had one athletic fuck session," Leon said. "Two club sandwiches, two cheeseburgers, two pieces of German chocolate cake, and two strawberry milkshakes."

"No," I said.

"At four forty-five, the hotel fire alarm activated and the building was evacuated. At five thirty-eight during a room sweep, your friend was found dead. We have enough," he said to Leon. "Let's call the police."

I put my face in my hands. I thought of the half avocado she'd eaten before. Her stomach.

"I wasn't there," I said in a whisper.

"I bet."

I told them about waking up in the middle of the night, going to the bathroom and finding myself locked outside in the hallway. I told them that I'd crept down the stairwell naked, all thirty-eight floors. I told them I'd pulled the fire alarm, out of embarrassment, when I couldn't attract the attention of the bellhop.

Neither Ron nor Leon spoke.

"That's how I left my pass card in her room. After the evacuation, I was let back in my room and I tried her on the phone but couldn't reach her. Actually, a man answered. You were there, weren't you. You know I called."

Ron was no longer talking to me. "The stairwell video," he said to Leon.

They left the room. The door locked. I slumped in the chair. I thought of her ordering all that food and began to cry.

Ron carried a suitcase when he returned to the room. Leon carried a bundle of clothes.

"We have no reason to keep you any longer, Mr. Franke," Ron said. "We've checked you out of your

room, and we have all of your belongings, we think, but please inspect them and make sure."

My suitcase on the desk. My suit folded neatly beside it. My shoes. My wallet and cell phone in a baggy resting on my suit.

"Tell me what happened to her?"

"The police are handling this."

Ron began to go over my belongings, lifting them for me to see.

"And from your room. Socks. Underwear. Book. Shaving kit. And a complementary robe for all guests inconvenienced by the fire alarm."

"Even though you were the cause of that inconvenience," Leon said.

I watched Ron lift each item in turn and place it in my suitcase.

"May I have my cell phone, please." I held out my hand.

Ron passed it to me.

"Leon will help you leave the hotel," Ron said. "If you don't mind. We'd rather you didn't go through the lobby."

I followed Leon two steps behind, suitcase following on rollers.

The hallway dead-ended. Leon pushed open a creaking door, and flicked a switch on the inside wall. The lights burst into brightness and then wavered, oscillating between dimness and glare.

"Where are we?" I said.

I saw metal counter tops and stoves, cupboards and shelves, decrepit as an abandoned building.

The countertops were scratched with grooves of rust. The shelves were sagging. There were swept-up piles of dust on the concrete floor and a tray full of utensils scattered across a long table.

I felt Leon's hand on my shoulder and his hand come across my mouth.

"Hold still," he said.

I threw myself forward out of his grasp, fell to the floor, scrambled to my feet and immediately ran into a metal table. Cutlery scattered in a cascade of noise.

"Goddamn it," Leon said.

He was on me in the next moment, pulling me down from behind, knees into my back, arm wedging my face to the floor. I twisted around beneath him and saw that he held a gun in his hand and that he was trying to aim it at my head.

"What are you doing?" I yelled. I stabbed upward with whatever had made its way into my hand and saw Leon's face explode in red, a hole punched into his cheek.

"Fuck *me*!" Leon said, as blood shot from his face.

I swung again, this time striking Leon in the neck.

On his knees, his throat in his free hand, the gun dangling.

"Why?" I yelled.

I had a spoon in my hand. A spoon, used the right way, was a prison weapon of choice.

I kicked him over and drove it into his torso. The spoon slid into the flesh of his stomach. He tried to squirm away.

"What did you do to her!?"

I stabbed again, even as Leon began to flail violently, a switch turned on, electricity ripping him alive. I kept stabbing into the soft spot, smacking wetly down, his shirt souping up. I could taste the muck in my mouth.

"Oh my God, Frank! What are you doing?"

The bellboy stood above me. I looked up at him when my vision cleared.

"Meeks?"

He did not have the ponytail. He was scrubbed clean and dressed in a prim uniform. But I recognized him now.

"Oh my God," he said. "Oh my God."

"He was trying to kill me." My voice rasping, something torn in my throat.

"Get out of here. Run."

And when I didn't move:

"Go!"

5

It was late morning. I walked down Madison, suitcase rolling behind me. I had washed my face and hands in a Starbucks restroom, changed my shirt. I could not, however, get the taste of blood out of my mouth, a grit of putrid mud. I felt that I should hurry, that I should get out of the daylight but my pace was sluggish and almost drunken, and it was difficult to successfully avoid those rushing by. My eyes were so sensitive to the light that I squinted painfully at any glimpse of bright objects, the glint of car metal, the glass of buildings. My hand trembled uncontrollably when I took out my phone to look at the screen. I wanted Kiedler to call, to text, to email, to tell me what to do. Instead, I saw the texts from her.

"Where are you?" at 3:48 A.M.

"I need you," at 3:51.

Above all, I needed sleep. But I did not know where to go, how to find refuge. I could not go back to San Diego. Nothing for me there or anywhere. I could not stay in a respectable hotel. I needed to hide.

But where do you hide in New York? Manhattan was a self-contained world, a Disney theme park for the monied and the elite. I drained my credit card at three different ATMs, then found a room in a genuine flop house on the Bowery.

It was the smallest room I'd ever stayed in. A slender appendage of hallway, a narrow cut of bed, a chunk of dresser with a drawer that hung half open, like a dead tongue.

I did not know what to do with Leon's gun. I stared at it, remembering the way it had looked when it was pointed directly at my head. How I had reacted. How quickly such a terrible thing had come to pass. It frightened me to think that I could end my troubles so easily now. Finally, I tucked it under the mattress.

I crawled onto the bed in my clothes and huddled there, and when the trembling subsided, I actually fell asleep.

Whenever I woke, I checked my phone.

Kiedler will call. Kiedler will tell you what to do.

Kiedler didn't call.

I kept trying him, of course, but no answer. I didn't leave a message or send a text. I feared leaving more of a trace than I was already doing.

For two days, I did not leave my room except to use the bathroom at the end of the hall. It had been years since I'd seen cigarette butts at the bottom of a urinal. What drove me out, finally, was hunger. I woke from a dream in which my stomach was being ripped open by steel claws. When I came to

consciousness, the pain was still with me, and a rash had spread all over my belly, like measles but with white pustules at each red dot, as though I'd become covered with ingrown hairs, but I knew it was hunger that had really stirred me up. I dressed, stumbled into the hallway, and escaped the building, pausing dizzily on the stoop. I looked around for police but it was only an ordinary day, warmer than it had been before, the street thronged, as always, with people. I found a Chinese restaurant on the next block and ate two goopy, sauce-soaked meals, then, still ravenous but fearing the need for other sorties to the contaminated outer world, bought bottles of water, a tabloid newspaper, and more food—a loaf of bread, a jar of Nutella, a bag of cookies, a box of jelly-filled granola bars, a dozen cans of cheap tuna fish—and brought it all back to my room. I collapsed on the bed, stared at the ceiling, and slept some more without realizing that my eyes had closed, my thoughts dissolving into darkness.

When I awoke this time, it was because I was crying. I sat on the bed with sweat-soaked sheets wound around my legs, unwrapped my loaf of bread, and ate and cried and ate.

My phone remained inert, a useless device, a dead and mute thing. When I checked the email accounts I had used with Kiedler and Amanda, I saw that they were empty. The text messages too were gone. As if they'd never been. I wondered if they ever had.

The numbness of my shock was dissolving, leaving me in an agitated state. An anger began to

burn within me, and I wondered how long before it went volcanic.

I could not stop thinking about her. I could not stop wondering.

I found the book in my suitcase and sat on the edge of the bed.

The garish cover, the buxom beauty in the red bikini running out of the jungle toward the beach, the tall Cary Grant type in the business suit aiming his long barrelled pistol at some distant threat. Peering closer, I saw in the foreground what he must be aiming at. On the beach, crawling from the water, a lizard rising up on all fours as if it might stand. *Attack of the Sea Monkeys* by Gadsen Wells.

I opened the cover to look for the inscription.

Grace, I would defend you in your
bikini against an army of sea monkeys!
Love,
Peter

At first, I could not understand the words, as though I'd lost the ability to read. In my brain, I'd been looking for the phrase she had read aloud to me—*"I yearn for you, Amanda. I am your knight in grey-suited armour. Nev."*—and when I did not see it, I found that the string of letters jumbled along dyslexically until I sorted them out and said them aloud. I felt the most irrational panic overwhelm me, a sense that I had caused a great wrong. Had I taken the wrong book? Was that the reason why the world had been shaken and twisted like the scenery in a kaleidoscope? I ran through the plausible possibilities even as I

knew, on a rational level, that this was in fact the book that Amanda had shown me in her room and said was a present from Moss, inscribed to her. The book I'd snuck from her nightstand to look at more closely in the bathroom. The book I'd held in front of my genitals as I made my way to the hotel lobby. The book the security guards had returned to me in itemized fashion among my belongings. The same book. Not transformed or replaced. Yet the inscription she had read to me was gone. Or had I misunderstood her words or had she lied?

I lay back on my thin mattress. In the logic of my nightmare, I knew that by stealing the book from her sleeping side I had broken a spell, banished my princess to some terrible place she would never escape.

I opened the book again a few hours later, still sick to my stomach, still desperate but newly determined to understand. The author, Gadsen Wells, was familiar but I could not think of why I knew the name. There was no picture, and very little information about him on the back, only that he was a novelist and scientist living in New York with his wife and their two Dachshunds, Knobby and Fritz. The book was published by Red River Press in 1972.

I started to read and did not stop until I was done.

The story was set in the South Pacific on an island called Rui Nodo. An oil company had drilled deeper than it should, and discovered a race of sentient sea monkeys who lived beneath the island. The sea monkeys wanted to take over the world.

I wrapped the book tightly in a plastic convenience store bag and stuffed it into the inside pocket of my sports jacket. I stepped over a drunk on the stoop, like a movie extra dead from some horrible plague. I looked like a drunk myself, unshaven, unwashed, my clothes loose, my skin flaking and blotchy. I tried not to look around in any paranoid way, but my eyes darted. I peered for shadows, for cops, for glints of rifle barrels sticking out of windows half-ajar. I walked toward the library at Bryant Park.

Along the way, I checked my phone one last time. No messages. It had come to me in the middle of the night that my cell had stopped being a device for connection and had turned into a bar code that followed me everywhere. I saw an open grating and dropped the phone. It landed with a clatter, bounced and spun, then caught on the grating perched on the edge of oblivion. I nudged it with my toe toward the gap between the iron teeth and saw it slip over the edge without a sound.

A young business woman hurried her pace as she walked by, a look of confusion on her face, as if I had dropped my pants and squatted to defecate.

At the library, the terminals were all in use by a huddled army of the homeless, the unemployed, the vaguely ill. I looked about and did not know where to go, how to proceed. Finally, I saw a librarian, a slender man in his forties, wearing a cardigan and a name tag, frowning over a stack of books.

I approached him. My voice croaked and sounded strange even to my own ears. I cleared my throat and tried again.

"How can I find out some information about an old book?"

I could tell he saw me as a homeless or near homeless user of the facilities, the kind who trolled for hours every day on the open terminals, and probably fouled the restrooms. He dealt with me politely, however, as if a memo had insisted he should.

"Have you looked it up on the computer?"

I shrugged and looked around at the rows of computers, all occupied.

"If you're not here by nine, you're lucky to get any access all day."

When this response did not shake me from his sight, he relented.

"Why don't I look it up for you?"

I nodded, and told him the name of the book and the name of the author, reluctant to show the book with its lurid cover. I saw his eyebrow arch a micro-fraction as I spoke, certain now that I was wasting his time.

"I don't see anything in our files," he announced, after clicking through a number of portals. "Are you sure you have the right title and author?" Dubious that I did.

"I'm sure."

"If we don't have it, or have a record of it, I'm afraid it probably doesn't exist," the librarian said.

"It exists," I said. I pulled the paperback from my inner coat pocket, unwrapped it from the plastic bag, and placed it carefully on the counter. The librarian looked at it without touching, then leaned forward.

"Neat," he said. "Do you mind if I open it?" Cautious about how a deranged man might react to having his precious stuff touched.

"Go ahead," I offered.

"Well, it clearly exists. And it certainly looks as though it's professionally published. I love the cover."

I nodded.

"No ISBN but that makes sense for copyright 1972."

He picked up a pencil and scribbled information on a scrap of paper, what looked like title, author, publisher, year. He picked the book up, turned it around several times, read the opening, flipped through it, glanced at other pages, handed it back.

"I'll see what I can find out. Why don't you visit again in an hour."

I thanked him. I took the book back and wrapped it awkwardly in the plastic, conscious that I was being watched. Then I turned around to face the library and look for an empty computer.

I didn't find one, of course. It seemed that no one had come to the library for books, only for the Internet. People read more in prison. I sat at one of the few tables that did not have a computer and wondered what to do. I glanced at the librarian. He did not glance back. He'd said an hour, I reminded myself. Would he call the cops? I knew it was an irrational fear but I pondered it just the same. I was warm in my jacket. I felt sleepy and overexerted, anxious. I did not have the energy, however, to leave my spot and search for a book, nor did I want to extract the

sea monkey novel from my pocket and read it again. Like a homeless man, I trusted no one. There was, however, a messy pile of newspapers in the middle of the table. I had not read a newspaper in a week. Would Amanda be inside? Her mysterious death in a hotel bathroom? What about the hotel security guard? Would my picture be in the paper? With a trembling hand, I reached for the pile and dragged it toward me across the table. Various newspapers, various dates. I took my time flipping pages. I was having trouble focussing. An almost sedative-like fatigue had come over me as though I had been overexposed to the stimulus of the world. I plodded on page after page, fighting a dense migraine.

On the third issue of the *Wall Street Journal*, I found a story that unravelled whatever reality I had been living in.

The librarian touched my shoulder. The same librarian as before. He looked at me with concern.

"Are you alright?"

I did not answer, merely stared.

"Your book," he said. "As I suspect, we have nothing on it. The Library of Congress site does have it listed, however. But there's not even a digital scan available. Did you find it on the street?"

I continued to stare.

"I can't find anything more about the author. It's possible, of course, that Gadsen Wells is a pen name. The publisher, Red River Press, is defunct. We do have a few other books published by them, but they've been pulled from circulation. If you give me a few days, I could probably find them. Would you like me to look?"

I nodded.

"They're terrific titles. *Revolution by Air Ship. Barrels Full of Vengeance.*"

He waited—for my approval, I suppose. I said nothing.

"I had an idea. There's a guy in the Village who's an expert on pulp fiction. I bet if you brought him this book he could tell you something about it. I've written down his address."

He handed me a piece of paper.

"Thank you," I said.

I left without saying another word.

Outside, at the top of the stone steps, I started to shake. I found a clear space below one of the grand lions, and huddled there as though freezing.

According to the Journal, the CEO of Xcelsion, Neville Moss, had been killed in the crash of a small private airplane over the Sierras, between San Diego and New Mexico. The plane had been en route to a private air strip near Taos. The destination was an exclusive wellness centre named Saffron Hills. The debris of the plane was difficult to reach and scattered over a wide distance.

Among the executives on board was Kevin Kiedler of Xcelsion Energy. Another was Amanda Barden of Chapek Energy.

Shares in both firms were down at the end of trading.

The initial article was perfunctory, subdued, though loaded with accolades for Moss and his

accomplishments, as well as some acknowledgement of his difficult personality, his take-no-prisoners approach. The subsequent articles revelled in speculation. Why had a senior Chapek executive been on board a flight with the CEO of Xcelsion?

Xcelsion and Chapek denied persistent rumours that secret merger negotiations had been ongoing.

I wandered the streets for hours, the hatch-work labyrinth a maze I felt compelled to trace. I was too confused to care about being discovered.

Saffron Hills was not on the island of Rui Nodo in the South Pacific. It was in New Mexico.

Amanda Barden was not the woman I had slept with at the hotel.

Kiedler's widow was my ex-wife. His daughter my ex-daughter.

I lay on my bed, as I felt I was supposed to, and stared at the ceiling. But I did not cry and I was not devastated.

I was beyond all of that.

A weightlessness had come over me. A sense that a curtain had been lifted.

Everything was a fiction.

I thought of dutiful Kiedler helping out good-naturedly at our home when my ex-wife and I hosted team parties. I thought of my ex-wife listening intently when I talked about Kiedler and his limitations, his absence of guile, his lack of a killer instinct.

Had the affair begun when Kiedler worked for

me? Kiedler dutiful and good-natured, secretly screwing her. Did it happen after I went to prison? Kiedler comforting her, profiting in my absence. What had she seen in Kiedler that she had not seen in me?

I remembered the pain of my marriage, the bitter anger that had grown within me over its insufficiencies, the solace I'd found in gambling. I remembered how bereft I was after she informed me, through her lawyer, that she was bringing it to an end, how lonely and abandoned that had left me, and how distraught I'd been over the changing of my daughter's last name. How I acquiesced, for her own good, because of my shame.

I rose from the bed, found the note the librarian had given me, and shoved the paperback into my jacket pocket.

The address was a basement apartment in the West Village. I walked down three steps to an iron grate set into a brick arch. The grate squeaked as I swung it open. Behind was an ordinary wooden door, and a brass plate that read: "The Pulpery."

I knocked and there was no answer. I turned the door knob and found it locked. I saw a doorbell and pressed and heard a chime.

Slow steps. A scuffle before the door. I sensed that I was being gazed upon. I pulled my hand from my pocket and held up the book in the plastic bag. Nothing changed. I unwrapped the plastic bag and held the book up again. A moment later, I heard the dead bolt retreat in its socket.

His name was Bartholomew Preston. Every wall of the apartment was lined with books. The colours were resplendent, the spines almost universally narrow. I inhaled the dust of a million forgotten stories.

Preston took my book and stared at the cover through thick glasses. His eyebrows were woolly and out of control. His fingertips and teeth were stained with tobacco.

"I've seen this," he said. "But not for years. I don't have a copy."

We entered what had once been a living room or a bedroom, still lined floor to ceiling with paperbacks. He stood before one of the shelves, ran his finger along it and edged out a corner, then asked over his shoulder.

"Do you want to sell it? I can give you thirty dollars."

"I want to contact the author."

Preston smirked, pulled out the book that he'd been fingering. "There is no such person. I know that much."

"A pen name?"

"Hmmm."

"Is there some way I can found out the author's real name?"

"You might be able to find someone who once worked at Red River Press, but I don't know how likely it is that they would remember one obscure author with an unusual pseudonym after forty years. Have you Googled it?"

"The librarian said that there were no other books in his name."

"I'm not talking about the catalogue listings, I'm talking about the Internet. Pen names are usually chosen deliberately. The authors are typically desperate for the money, but still proud, and this can make them sarcastic or ironic or even sentimental in the choice of pen name. If he was successful as a pulp writer he might have been a failure as a serious novelist or poet. Your Gadsen Wells probably had ten other names. This may have been a specific name for a specific purpose. He might have combined a couple names or used a maiden name and a father's middle name or taken it from his favourite war novel or from the Sears Catalogue."

"I'll look it up."

He opened the book again. "There's bound to be prose within it, idiosyncratic expressions that make it distinctive. You might be able to do a phrase analysis."

"What does that mean?"

"After the Unabomber, the FBI developed software to analyze writing tendencies across a database of documents. Not just books but speeches, essays, articles. I've been told it works. They've been able to identify kidnappers through ransom notes. Determine threat sources through emails."

"I don't really want to contact the FBI."

"Who would? I have a colleague in North Carolina who has access to the FBI database for his own research. His name is Adrian Hautman. You could hire him privately, though I imagine he would charge you more than thirty dollars."

A glance at my clothing.

"I can't go to North Carolina right now."

Preston shook his head as if I amused him.

"I'll give you his phone number."

When he returned to the room he handed me a card.

"Are you sure you won't sell? Seventy-five dollars."

"It means more to me than money."

Preston smiled. "Sad, isn't it, how much we love them."

I think he was talking about books.

I bought a new phone at a junk store on Canal Street, one with a limited number of pre-paid minutes, no registration needed. It was difficult to press the right buttons. In my room, I called Preston's colleague, Hautman, and when he answered and I told him who had referred me, I explained that I wanted to find out the true identity of a pulp fiction writer from the 1970s.

"Why?"

I was taken aback by the question.

"Why do you need to know why?"

"When someone wants to use me to track someone down I get to ask why. Are you a stalker? Does he owe you money? Did he drop your grandmother off at a back alley abortionist?"

This seemed both old-fashioned and deliberately provocative, as though he wanted to press my crazy button. Oddly, it only made me calmer. I could not tell him the truth, of course, but a lie came to me.

"I always suspected that my father wrote a novel. He died when I was young, and before my mother remarried she threw out all his old papers, except for one particular book which I found in her

belongings after she passed this year. There are some details in this book that remind me of him and the coincidences have become kind of an obsession for me. I'd like to know whether he wrote it or not."

"You don't have anything else that your father wrote? No letters, no diary?"

"Nothing."

I could tell he didn't believe me.

"What's his name?"

"I don't want to tell you that."

"You want me to sing for my supper."

"Something like that."

"Okay, send me the book, I'll run it through the database and see what comes up."

"I can't do that. I can't let it go."

A pause. "Do you have the book on you right now?"

"I do."

"Okay. Hold on. I'm going to record you. That's a legal notification, which I am bound by the criminal statute of the state of North Carolina to give. Open the book and start reading."

"Start reading?"

"Read the first few paragraphs."

I opened the book and began to read.

"That's enough," Hautman said, after I'd finished the third page.

So I stopped.

When I hung up I got off the bed and down on the floor and began to do push-ups. Then sit-ups. Then jumping jacks and squats. I did them until stars tingled in my vision.

I was losing my caution, overly comfortable with the indifference of New York and the invisibility of my new life. Then, the next morning, standing at a deli and sipping a coffee sweet with sugar and milk, I peered at the *Post* and saw that an antiquarian bookstore in the West Village, called the Pulpery, established in 1978, had been burned to the ground. In addition to the building, and adjacent apartments, tens of thousands of books had been lost. There was speculation that the proprietor, Bartholomew Preston, had been in financial difficulty.

I arrived at the library before nine, early enough to grab one of the terminals, cautious again, quick with my glances, ready to run. The librarian in the cardigan spotted me at a desk but I looked away. I wondered whether he knew about Preston. He did not look my way again. The terminals were almost immediately full. A few bums like myself. But also business men. Teenagers. Retirees. Housewives with children. A secret order of the harried, downtrodden, and luckless.

There were so many questions I wanted to ask the Internet, and so many answers I didn't want to learn.

Who was Amanda Barden—the Amanda I met in the hotel room—and who was the Amanda who died in the plane crash? When had Kiedler and my ex-wife gotten married? Why had Meeks been working as a bellboy in the hotel? Who was Gadsen Wells?

I spent my morning there and the better part of the afternoon. The only time I left the terminal was to use the bathroom and I paid a bum—a real

bum—to sit in my space until I got back.

Gadsen Wells was not a person, it turned out.

Gadsen Wells was a town in Wisconsin.

I found the name in a list of environmental disasters of the past century. *1950 Gadsen Wells spill* was all that it said.

I could find nothing on Google maps for Gadsen Wells, nor anything about it in any online history of Wisconsin, as if the Internet had blanked the town's existence.

My librarian friend was surprised to see me standing before him, agitated and harried. But he directed me to the basement where I found the microfiche library of old newspapers, the *Milwaukee Journal Sentinel* among them.

Nineteen-fifty seemed like the right year to start. I began in January, sifting through the events of each day, the microfiche making a peculiar fluttering sound when it gained speed, like a cockroach in flight. In May of 1950 I came across the first mention of Gadsen Wells and a reference to contamination in the local river. Then the mentions picked up in frequency until the town became the subject of a long piece, in August, which outlined its history as well. Located 60 miles southeast of Eau Claire, Gadsen Wells had been founded in the late 1800s by wildcatters out of Pennsylvania. The Wells had shown promise initially but the oil had proven too dirty with shale and sand to refine cheaply so the wildcatters and their money had moved on.

Then, in the 1940s, when oil prices spiked

because of the war, the drillers came back, but this time they wanted to free the oil by cracking the shale surrounding the deposits. It was a new technique, discovered by Germans and brought to Gadsen Wells by a first generation Czech-American named Vladimir Chapek. Chapek had made a fortune in the '20s through a variety of industrial companies, paper and pulp mills, copper mines, as well as other businesses, like a toilet bowl and sink manufacturer, a newspaper in Chicago, and a dime store publishing house in New York. But he had repatriated to Moravia when his American businesses went bankrupt during the Great Depression, decrying the communism that was taking over the country via FDR. His interests in Europe were confiscated at the beginning of World War II, so he returned to the US and started a company called Midwest Petroleum to test out the new technologies of oil extraction which, the article implied, he'd more or less stolen from a German company operating in the Sudetenland. He was considered a hero for having done this on behalf of market capitalism. To find the right place to drill, Chapek followed the old wildcatters of the previous century, men who'd swarmed Titusville, Pennsylvania when oil was discovered there, abandoned it when the oil went dry, and moved west through Ohio, Oklahoma, and even California looking for the next strike. In Gadsen Wells, Chapek found the right conditions for his technology and turned the town from a sleepy hollow of thirty or forty residents into a thriving producer of shale oil over night, and a bit of a boom town. It was said

that Wisconsin would be the new Oklahoma.

Then, in June 1950, a thick slurry suffused the nearby river, suffocating its surface, clogging its nooks, tarring its banks. The trout population was decimated immediately. The shoreline turned from a lush green to a scorched grey within days. Even after the river water cleared out, the slurry stuck to the banks. Midwest Petroleum promised to improve the river by bringing in work crews to strip the affected soil, but the problem, it seemed, was spreading, the slurry showing up in other creeks, in wells, and even appearing in the bubbles that ran from natural springs.

Over the following months, there were more stories about Gadsen Wells, mostly concerning the number of people who had become sickened by the fumes that wafted over the town on still evenings. The locals blamed the drilling, but Midwest Petroleum denied any responsibility. A town ordinance banning further drilling within a fifty-mile radius was defeated in the state legislature.

"This is a plague," one resident declared, "and no one in Madison cares."

By August 1951, according to the next article, the town had been reduced from 8,000 residents to nine. Those nine refused to leave despite a federal order declaring the area uninhabitable. "We've finally got the place to ourselves," retired truck driver and World War II Veteran Arthur Krauss said from his front porch, with wife Deborah. "We're comfortable here, and we're not going anywhere."

I searched through another year of newspapers but found nothing more.

When I went back upstairs to the terminals, I saw that the bum I'd paid previously was occupying his own computer now. I clapped him on the back and said, "Thanks."

He protested but I gave him a ten this time, just to smooth over the hurt.

I knew what to look for now. In 1968, I found a reference to Gadsen Wells in a scientific study of the long-term impact of the slurry on the southwest portion of the state. The researchers had found the trout population resilient but had discovered that a species of giant salamander had become extinct. The common name was Hellgoat Salamander, the scientific name *sphenomorphus* skink, but the locals referred to it as a "king devil," "mud lunger," or "water monkey." Researchers described it as the largest amphibian in the northern United States, previously only known to have existed in South America, and thought to have occupied the region relatively undisturbed for 65 million years.

Locals weren't so certain that the Hellgoat was gone.

"They bury themselves in the mud, those king devils, and sleep for years and years," said one sports fisherman who complained that the salamander had always been a bigger threat to the trout than any slurry. Another offered the opinion that the reason the trout were thriving now was that the king devils were sleeping or dead. "Either that, or the earth opened up and they swam back to hell where they belong," he added.

I was surprised by the size of the creature. In the black and white photo, a captured salamander

was hoisted in the arms of a fisherman like some giant catfish, almost two feet long, with frog-like skin. It had oddly short appendages with agile-looking fingers and toes, and a strange tufted ridge on its chin that resembled a beard. According to the text box, the beard was probably used for sensory perception in lightless underwater crevices.

Of course, I could not help but think of the sea monkeys described in Gadsen Wells's book.

I called my old job the next morning, the call centre in Eau Claire. It had only been three months since I'd worked there, but it seemed like lifetimes ago, or different lives, lived by other me's. It took nine calls and eight hang ups to reach Cal. I recognized his voice as soon as he answered.

"Frank!" he boomed, when I mentioned it was me, and then his voice went hushed as if he realized that some other son of a bitch was probably taking note of his personal call that very moment.

"What are you doing calling about benefits?"

I explained that I wasn't calling about benefits, I was calling about something strange, something very important, something possibly critical to the security of the state. That got Cal's full attention.

"Have you heard of a town called Gadsen Wells?" I asked.

Cal said that he was not familiar with any such a town.

"It used to be about sixty miles southeast of Eau Claire," I told him, "but it's been abandoned for over fifty years."

"How come?"

"Some European oil company poisoned it."

It wasn't true, but nor was it completely false. However, I wanted to motivate Cal in the most direct way.

"GDSOBs," Cal said.

"I wonder if you could ask around, discreetly, and see if anyone knows anything about it."

"Why?"

"I'm doing an investigation," I hesitated, as though there was more to say, but I was not at liberty to say it.

"What kind of investigation?"

"Into big business," I said. "That's the work I do. I'm kind of a spy."

"No shit," Cal said.

I hoped that this confirmed his long-held suspicions over my unlikely employment at the call centre.

"Can I count on you?" I asked.

"Piece of cake, brother, piece of cake."

I knew I needed to get another room, switch flop houses, maybe change my jacket, grow a beard. But after I returned to my room and did my exercise routine, I did not have the motivation to pack up and leave.

I could only lay on my bed and think.

I thought about Kiedler and my wife. I thought about a plane that had gone down over the Sierras, the remains of five passengers and three crew still unrecovered. I thought about Chapek and Xcelsion and secret merger talks. I thought about the other Amanda Barden, the one I'd texted with for months,

murdered in the hotel. I had the feeling that I was meant to die in that hotel room, too, that I had been set up to be in the room with her when they came for her.

If not for the book. My need to see it more closely, and my mistake in opening the hallway door instead of the bathroom door, I would have been with Amanda when they entered. Had she struggled? Had they killed her by surprise? I thought about my own fight in the old kitchen, the suddenness of my instinct for viciousness. I could still taste the mucky blood in my mouth. I saw Meeks standing above me. "What have you done?"

What had I done?

There was a horror to it, and a power.

I stared at the ceiling in wonder.

Adrian Hautman called me the next morning. In his curtness he sounded anxious to end the call as quickly as possible, even fearful. I remembered Bartholomew Preston and could grasp the reason, but that slowed me down in my understanding of what Hautman was telling me. I had to ask him to repeat himself and he hesitated, as though he suspected something in my delay, perhaps a trace being put on his call. His frustration with me and maybe his bitterness overcame his caution and reluctance, however, and he spit it out again.

"The passage you read to me correlates to two items in the public digital record. One, a book published in 1970; the other, a letter to the editor of the *New York Times* written in 1979. In fact there are several phrases verbatim. It would be tagged for

plagiarism, but I suspect the same person wrote both items and your dime-store novel."

"What's the book from 1970?" I asked, my heart fluttered through my shirt.

"It's called *The Leadership Game: How to Leverage Power in Pursuit of Your Agenda*. It's by a man named Vladimir Chapek, then Chairman of the Board of an energy company called Midwest Hastings. Your father?"

"No," I said. "What about the letter. Who wrote that?"

"Two people. Another CEO of Midwest Hastings, Neville Moss, and the CFO, Peter Stoddard."

I was silent.

"Mr. Frank. Are you satisfied with my research?"

"Yes," I said.

"Then please don't call me again."

He hung up.

I shaved in the bathroom at the end of the hall. I cut my nails. I washed myself thoroughly in the sink using cleaning rags and a chunk of soap.

When I returned to my room, I found a man on his hands and knees, peering under my bed.

Meeks.

He tried to stand and launch himself at me as soon as I entered but he tripped on the corner of the bed and by the time he reached me he was falling more than attacking. It was not difficult to wrestle him to the floor. When I had wedged his face into the carpet for long enough, he begged me to stop.

I kicked the door shut behind me.

"Sit in the corner," I said, and dragged him by the collar and bent wrist toward the wall and threw him down. Then I lifted the mattress and found the gun. A miracle he hadn't found it first.

"Looking for this?" I said.

He shook his head. His lips were swollen and red.

"I need the book," he said.

I did not let the surprise show on my face.

"Why? Because it links them?"

"You don't want to do this, Frank. We're on the same side."

"What side is that?"

"Her side."

"Her?"

"Samantha. I mean Amanda. Her real name is Samantha."

I could not take this in. There was only pain at the mention of her name.

"Who are you, Meeks? Why have you destroyed my life?"

He started to speak and then stopped.

I lifted the gun and pointed it at his face.

"Frank," he said.

I waited.

"I'm an activist," he said.

"Do you mean an environmental activist?"

He nodded.

"I'm with Carbon Audit."

I sat on the edge of the bed, the gun still in my hand but pointed away from him now, less threatening, less direct.

"Start from the beginning. The day you walked into my office and showed me how to cover my online activities. Why did you do that?"

"We were looking for leverage on the company. You had unrestricted access to the personnel files of the top executives at Xcelsion. The exclusion portal I showed you allowed us to track all the work you were doing. We didn't mean for you to get caught. We wanted to use you for years. But you, you couldn't help yourself—" He stopped.

"Believe me, Meeks, I take full responsibility for my personal weaknesses."

He wiped his forehead and then looked at me as though worried about how I would react to that sudden movement.

"You got us places, though, Frank, you really did. With your access we saw some illegal financial activity going on, clear instances of suppliers and vendors getting contracts they shouldn't have won, and with some work we were able to tie expense accounts and specific meetings and business trips to make most of the executive team look guilty. Then we handed the whole file to a DA on a memory stick."

"You're saying not everyone was guilty in that kickback scheme."

"Well, not everyone. At least three and possibly six guys. But they were all guilty of working for Xcelsion. The stock price fell by eighty-six percent. The assets got sold off at fire-sale prices. It was one of our biggest wins."

A win, I thought. Destroying a company. If the

gun were pointed at me, I'd have to confess to the same desire. To see it all crash and burn. And yet, I saw the futility of that now, and even more, the cost.

"As wins go, Meeks, it didn't last for long," I said. I put disdain into my voice, bitterness.

"They came back," Meeks nodded. "Like a fucking zombie. Neville Moss turned them around. He's not normal. He's a sociopath. He wouldn't stop. So we needed to figure out how to stop him, or at least control him. And we almost did, thanks to Samantha. She had surgery just to spend time in the wellness retreat where we knew he went. She won him over. We got enough pictures and video of them together to develop the story."

"What story?"

"That Xcelsion and Chapek were doing deals together, secretly. We built a website and had it primed for launch. We were going to show reporters before anything became official, leak the news and let pandemonium break out. A joint venture we called X-Alt. Catchy name, right? Chapek's deep sea fracking technology, Xcelsion's project finance in the worst of the third world. And then we were going to link it all back to the earthquake in the South Pacific, the drilling rig blowing up, the salamanders gone extinct, executives killed by terrorists. We wanted something CNN and Fox would argue over for weeks."

"You got the idea from the book."

"Moss told Samantha it was his favourite thriller. He was such an ass. But the idea was perfect and

he'd know where it had come from, and that she betrayed him when the story came out, but he wouldn't be able to say a thing on his own without risking complete humiliation."

"You're insane, Meeks."

"It would have worked, Frank, if Americans gave a shit when disasters happen overseas. That's the problem. We should have gone bigger, said a hundred thousand people were killed. Showed them what dirty energy really costs."

"You think business is a conspiracy, Meeks. There is no conspiracy. It's just business."

Meeks's eyes widened. He shifted on the ground as though he'd almost forgotten that a gun was pointing at him. "The conspiracy is business, Frank. Every lie we told has led to more truth. They're meeting right now, you know. The merger we made up is taking place."

"Who?"

"Chapek. Xcelsion. At the hotel. A hotel that Xcelsion owns. That's why I was there. Do you want to know all the other assets Xcelsion controls under how many different shell companies? Do you want to know how many politicians Xcelsion has paid off? The conspiracy is bigger than business. The conspiracy is America."

I pointed the gun at his face. "Who's meeting, Meeks? I want names."

"Stoddard's there. Kiedler's there. A handful of executives. A SEAL Team of lawyers. And Samantha's there, too. She's inside Chapek now, working undercover. "

"You're lying. And Kiedler's dead. He was killed in a plane crash."

"The plane crash was faked."

"You fake plane crashes, too."

"We didn't fake that. Xcelsion did."

"Jesus, Meeks, why the hell would they do that?"

"Because Neville Moss is dead. He died at his weekend house in Pescadero. Of a heart attack. Except they couldn't allow an autopsy. It would have all come out. His heart-lung transplant. The health conditions they'd hidden for over a year. So they faked the plane crash in a place where bodies go unrecovered all the time. They put Amanda Barden's name in there to clean up that other loose end and kill two birds with one stone. Prevent us from using her against Moss ever again."

"So why would they put Kiedler's name on your fake plane, too? That doesn't make any sense, Meeks. If you're right that Kiedler's at the hotel, he's still part of the gang."

"He is part of the gang. *I* put his name on that plane. To fuck up his plans. I hacked the first news story that came out about the crash, added his name to the list, and it stuck in every story afterward. Now Kiedler's the one in a jam."

I stood up and placed the gun on the dresser. For an instant, Meeks looked hopeful—he glanced at the gun and back at me—and then he saw me pull the sheet from the bed and begin to rip it into strips.

"What are you doing?" he asked.

"I think it's time we play a game," I answered.

"What do you mean? What kind of game?"

"The Prisoner's Dilemma. Do you want to know the rules?"

He grimaced and leaned back against the wall, weary. "I have a PhD in data analytics. I don't need you to explain game theory to me."

"I learned my game theory in prison, Meeks, as an actual prisoner. The book I read was very marked up. You could say game theory was a core part of the prison curriculum. It was the air we breathed. Who do you trust. Do you still trust them. Do you trust them now."

But not just prison. I remembered my wife clenching my hand under the table as we listened to my lawyer. *If you take this deal . . . if you don't . . .* How brutal the options had seemed to me, how fraught with risk. How little, it turned out, I'd actually understood.

"Except this game, Meeks, is not going to be theory," I said.

"I don't want to play any games, Frank. I'm too tired for games."

"You've just told me a story. And we both know you told it to me because you think it's your best bet for getting out of trouble. But I don't know if you made that bet by lying or telling the truth."

He stared at me.

"Fortunately, to make the game exciting, we know that at the other end of town, in that big suite at the Trident Hotel, there's a few other people who know the truth. Kiedler, if he's really alive. Maybe Stoddard. And when I ask someone over there the same questions that I asked you, they might tell me

a different story, in which case I'll know one of you is lying."

I picked up the gun again.

"So what will I do if that happens? I'm thinking, I'm just going to kill whoever I don't believe the most. That's how I'm feeling at the moment, anyway. But what does your game theory expertise tell you? Is that my likely decision?"

He looked pale, as though I'd already shot him, or as if he feared I'd completely lost my self-control.

"You're not the kind of person to kill someone, Frank. This is crazy."

"I've already killed someone. I stabbed him to death with a spoon. If there's anyone who shouldn't doubt me, it's you."

"He didn't die, Frank. He's fine. Well, I mean, after the surgery and the gastric bypass. But he's fine. I don't even think Leon holds a grudge."

I laughed. "Keep telling stories, Meeks. What I wonder, what I'm curious about, is in a situation like this, is it to your advantage to tell the truth or to tell a really good lie? And when I confront those others over there in Xcelsion's hotel, will you be better off if they confirm your story, or if they deny it to try and get the better of the deal?"

I took the rag I'd used to clean myself and balled it up and moved in close. He saw what I had in mind and began to move his head back and forth to avoid me, asking me not to, until I placed the muzzle of the gun square to his forehead and he became deathly still.

"Open up," I said.

He opened wide. I shoved the rag in.

"It really doesn't matter to me," I said, "whether you're an environmental activist or the single largest shareholder of Xcelsion stock. I pretty much hate all of you equally at this point."

I took a taxi to the hotel using Meeks's money. I had his bellhop passkey in my pocket. I wore my business suit, and though I felt like an imposter, the doorman held the door open for me and I strode into the lobby as if I were any other guest, or some business man arriving for a meeting.

I did not have the courage to go any farther.

The realization came over me like a wave of nausea. I began to shake and sweat, the anxieties of a lifetime pounding through every corpuscle in my body. I needed to steady myself against a wall to regain control over my breathing. I looked around. Someone would notice me for sure, in this state. Someone would divine my awful intentions. My murderous purpose. And they would summon help and swarm me and after I was restrained and subdued, piled on by security guards and stripped of my weapon, my only tool of power, they would connect me to the murder in the abandoned kitchen, too, and I would go back to prison to spend the rest of my miserable life alone, where I belonged.

Then I saw her.

Samantha.

Amanda.

Her.

She came in through the front doors just as I had. She wore a business suit, the same one I remembered from the flight we'd shared. She walked

alongside another business man. They both carried Starbucks coffees. She laughed with an ease I did not remember from before. They passed me, where I huddled pale and furtive against the wall near the gift shop, and strode toward the elevator bank. I followed at a distance, as though pulled along by her nearness. He pressed a button, and they waited. An elevator arrived quickly, and when its door slid open he held it for her with his free arm and gestured her in. She proceeded with an extravagant step forward, making a joke of his gallantry. They disappeared inside.

I stood there before the door, staring at it as if it were a portal into another life.

I watched the indicator light make quantum leaps from floor number to floor number, until it reached the thirty-eighth floor where Meeks had told me the meeting was taking place. Then it stopped and did not move any more.

Business is the conspiracy. America is the conspiracy.

My cell phone rang.

I stared at it. The number was not familiar.

It kept ringing. People glanced at me as I stared at the device in my hand. Finally, I answered.

"Frank."

It was a voice I didn't recognize.

"Who's this?"

I looked around, wondering whether the person calling me was also watching me.

"It's Cal. From Wisconsin."

"Cal," I said, as though he were my guardian angel. "Why are you calling?"

I walked out of the elevator bank to a quieter area near the piano.

"There's something going on there," Cal said. "Where Gadsen Wells used to be."

"What do you mean?"

"Some billionaire bought up the ghost town, all the buildings and roads, everything. And he's got a fence around it, and it's completely restricted. No access. But there's lights on all the time, apparently, and heavy equipment going in and out."

"Why would they do that?" I asked. My voice felt separate from me, like someone else was speaking in my place.

Cal hesitated, as if thrown by my nonchalant tone.

"Well, there's rumours."

"Are they drilling?" They had to be drilling.

"Some people say it's a theme park."

"A theme park?"

"Another rumour is that it's a zoo."

"A zoo?"

"Like a refuge," he said, "for some kind of endangered species. A lizard, if you can believe that. Some giant salamander, big as a catfish. You ever heard of anything as crazy as that?"

"You can't believe anyone anymore," I said.

"That's for sure," Cal said. "Me and a couple buddies are going down there this weekend to do a little reconnaissance. You want me to call you back with what I learn?"

"That would be great, Cal."

"Okay," he said, uncertain about how I was reacting to his plan.

"Cal?" I said. "Be careful."

"You, too," he answered.

I entered the elevator using Meeks's passkey for access.

I knocked on the door. Kiedler answered. He looked surprised. I pointed the gun into his chest, backed him up into the room, then swung it against his jaw. When he pulled himself together and sat up, between the bed and the TV, he had a grin on his face, an eager, satisfied expression.

"It's good to see you, friend," he said.

He struggled to stand up. I pressed the gun to his forehead to keep him down. He surrendered and sat back, arms at his side.

"Is there anyone else here?" I backed up and looked around the room. It was a large suite and I could not see it all. There was a closed door on the far wall.

He wiped his mouth. "They're in the next suite, getting ready for the big meeting. They could come in at any minute. Or I could yell. Call the troops."

"Stoddard?"

"And a dozen others. About seven lawyers if you need any representation."

"You work for him?"

"Not yet. I'm inconveniently dead. We haven't figured out how to handle that. Maybe I'll crawl out of the Sierras like a mountain man just in time for the merger announcement."

"Maybe I'll solve your problem. Can't kill a dead man."

"Good point."

"I've been talking to Meeks. You remember Meeks?"

"Sure. Updated my computer a dozen times."

That knowing grin.

"Meeks told me his story, and I promised him I wouldn't kill him if he was telling me the truth. Now it's your turn. But here's your dilemma." I wanted him to understand that I was in control, so I said it nice and slow. "You can lie to me and hope I won't know it's a lie. Or you can tell me the truth and hope I accept it. One of those strategies is likely to send me over the edge. And I promise you, this time I'm not going there alone."

He said nothing for a moment, just watched me as if assessing what I'd said. Then finally he spoke.

"Sounds like a rigged game to me. No wonder you lost so much money gambling."

I sat down on the corner of the bed, close enough to press the gun against him if I needed.

"The odds aren't totally stacked against you, Kevin. Maybe you can get yourself out of this jam that you're in."

His smile faded. I could see worry or fear or whatever bothered someone like Kiedler working its way through his system.

"I get it, Frank. I understand. It seems to me the cleanest way to win is to prove Meeks lied."

I shrugged. "Not sure yet. Try me out."

"Did he tell you the environmental story?" Kiedler asked "Carbon Audit. Saving the world from oil companies?"

"Who knows? Maybe."

"If he did he's lying. You can go shoot him now."

His confidence had returned as though he'd figured out some leverage to use. I could not help but be impressed.

"Alright, Kiedler, if Meeks is lying, it's time for you to tell me the truth."

"Let me sit up."

"No."

The gun against his forehead again.

He sank back, this time as much irritated as scared.

"You always were petulant, Frank. That was the worst thing about you. On the surface you were as gung ho as any of us, but I could tell you hated your job. Like work was distasteful. Like it was pulling its best from you and giving you nothing in return. That's a very shitty way to live. You had the talent and the brains to get promoted, but you lacked the authenticity to sustain it."

Kiedler knew me well enough still to stir the bitterness inside.

"You're not telling me anything I'm interested in hearing. Tell me about Carbon Audit."

"You have a need to understand. I get it. That was always a strong point. You may be disdainful but you're curious. You're a complicated guy, Frank."

I raised the gun slightly, and watched the door to the other room out of the corner of my eye. Was Kiedler stalling while someone in the next room called the police?

"Carbon Audit," I repeated.

"Carbon Audit isn't an anonymous environmental

activist group," Kiedler said. "That's their cover. They're actually a corporate investigation firm specializing in the energy industry."

"Bullshit," I said.

"You don't believe me. But I'm going to tell you anyway. They penetrate energy companies as employees, typically in HR or IT because of easy access to files and offices. They determine where security is being breached internally, who's embezzling, who's fixing contracts, who's trading on inside information, who's having an affair with the client or the vendor or the competition, and they make a report. Something is always going on in every big company. It's only a matter of finding out where. CA identifies the source and neutralizes it before it blows up into the kind of problem that will cost billions."

"If that's your story, why did Meeks approach me? I wasn't doing anything wrong."

"No, but he thought you were. Your behaviour had veered so far from your normal baseline, he started watching you closely."

"My baseline? I was having personal problems. Marital problems."

Kiedler knew all about my marital problems. But he continued as though the matter was academic.

"Meeks realized that later. But whenever someone alters their routine drastically for a period of time, comes to work earlier than usual, leaves later, makes fewer phone calls or more business trips, changes their private email address, those behaviours pop out of the data stream. Nine times out of ten, the level of sustained variation you showed means

embezzlement. He assumed you were one of them. I'm sure he's very sorry about that."

"One of who?"

"One of the executives in on the kickback scheme."

"That happened after I went to prison."

Kiedler grinned. "It had been going on for years, and it was so pervasive that it crossed almost every division. Meeks was looking for a common node, an organizer. You were in perfect position. Working with executives across silos. Access to secure personnel records, even expense accounts."

I laughed. The sound burst from my chest. "I was doing my job!"

"I know. And you were good at it. But the amazing thing, the miracle really, is that you catalyzed every other good that came later. There's something rare about that, something invaluable. The board begged Neville to come back. Someone from the old regime would have swept the problems under the rug. Neville cleaned house. Severed the past from the present. Made Xcelsion strong again. He was a great man. You were lucky to have spent so much time with him. I know he thought the world of you."

"If you admired him so much why the fuck did you betray him? Those emails and texts between him and Amanda Barden. You were trying to trap him, to force him into something he didn't want to do. Did Chapek pay you off? Promise you a cut?"

"I wasn't trying to trap Neville, I was trying to prod him."

"Prod him into what?"

"Into doing what's right for the company.

Xcelsion needs to change. It needs to shift its culture and business model, its values. Away from old technology and crude, into alternatives and a better diet of gas, solar, and even algae-based fuels. You'd be amazed what can be done, how close we are to the brink of a new world. That's where Chapek is going, but they lack the financial muscle and the assets to get there on their own. On paper, a merger makes more than just business sense, it could make a real difference for our future. The only thing stopping it was Neville's personal animosity toward Peter. I knew Neville hated Peter not out of spite or disdain but out of love. And Samantha was helping to open him up to that understanding. It would have worked if the SEC hadn't started to investigate the email exchanges. I brought you in to falsify that trail and give us the deniability to prevent an arraignment. But the merger, Frank, the merger was too vital to stop. Neville was ill. He didn't have much left for daily operations. I just wanted him to kick himself upstairs into the Chairman role and bring Peter in as CEO. That was the plan, anyway. Now we go forward without him."

"A Chapek Xcelsion merger."

"X-Alt. A new kind of energy company. A reality changer."

"What about my wife, Kiedler? What about that merger? My little girl. You prick. You piece of shit. You son of a bitch."

"That's erroneous, Frank. I don't know how the hell it got in that news article. And then it stuck in every article after. I'm single. I've got no time for a

family. And Allie is in San Francisco married to a VP at Yahoo. But instead of blaming me or her for what happened, why don't you look at your contribution? Do you honestly think an affair wasn't going to happen with someone? You destroyed your marriage a long time before you went to prison. You had nothing left for her when you got home at the end of every day. You were a shell. She was devastatingly lonely."

It was this beyond anything else that I could not bear to hear. I pressed the gun against his forehead, my hand was shaking, my voice had risen.

"I don't believe you!" I yelled. "I don't believe anything you've told me!"

The door opened. I'd forgotten about the people on the other side. I woke up from this moment, from the all-consuming anger, and felt embarrassed, as much as anything, to be standing there with tears in my eyes holding a gun to Kiedler's head.

I looked over and saw the man I knew was Peter Stoddard. He was tall. He wore a dark blue suit. He had dark hair that must have been dyed, or perhaps it was thicker because of hair implants. But he was a vital presence. A physical warping of the energy field in the room. Someone you looked to and waited for because he was suddenly standing there.

"Frank," he said, a voice that was calm but clear. "I know you're dealing with a lot at this moment. But I was wondering if I could talk to you before you do anything we will all regret. Do you mind?"

He stood back, and beckoned me toward his room.

I looked at Kiedler. I saw the doubt and fear in his eyes. He'd covered it up with bluster, but he knew I was capable of shooting him, where he huddled on the carpet between the bed and the TV.

In some ways, for whatever reason, that was enough.

I lowered the gun and walked toward Stoddard.

Stoddard allowed me to step by him into the room. I saw a board table, a couch, a number of soft chairs, a stunning floor-to-ceiling window along one wall, Manhattan outside. I saw a dozen people. Frozen. Staring at me. Terrified, I suppose, by the deranged man in a suit holding a handgun. They were only calm because Stoddard was calm. I saw Samantha among them. She had a different kind of fear in her eyes. The fear of discovery. The fear of being caught in a lie. I could not bear to look at her.

"Folks. Do you think you'd mind giving us twenty minutes? I know we're in the middle of these details. But sometimes life is important enough to interrupt."

At his words, they rose, wary but still calm. Took their smart phones. Their pens. A jacket. A purse. Filed past me, looking down, fearful, ashamed, embarrassed for me, relieved to be escaping. Stoddard closed the door behind them.

He turned to me. "It's early for a drink. But I'd have one with you. Or coffee. Or tea. Or a Vitamin Water. It's all here. Are you hungry?"

I did not know if I was hungry. I did not want anything. I could not think of any needs.

"Why don't you sit?"

He gestured toward one of the soft living room chairs. I sat and sank into the cushion. I felt exhausted but also exposed, like a circuit behind broken plastic.

Stoddard leaned against the board table and folded his arms, five feet from me. Nothing stern in the gesture. He was comfortable with himself and with the responsibility he was taking. I could see his eyes clearly. He did not waver in looking at me.

"I listened to Kevin speaking to you through the door," he began. "Most of what he said is true. I wouldn't have delivered the message in quite that way. But you guys have a complicated history and that makes it difficult to communicate with the right amount of consideration and caring. I understand."

I didn't understand, and then I did. "You're talking about you and Neville Moss."

Stoddard nodded. "We were like brothers. We got angry with each other because we cared about each other. We fought each other until someone or something else got in the way, then we fought that together. But the biggest thing we argued over was right and wrong. He had a good heart. But Neville was corrupted by the nature of the game. He liked winning more than he valued doing good."

He frowned, some regret or frustration come over him, and then he went on.

"After we split, I was consumed by our rivalry for too many years. I measured my own success against Neville's. When my business failed, I felt ten times the failure because Neville had not failed. When Neville

failed, it made everything I'd ever accomplished that much sweeter. It was such a waste. A waste of energy and emotion and friendship. I wish we could have reached out to each other one more time. This merger. Well, we might have fought all over again if we had to sit on the same board, but it might have been fun, too."

He smiled.

"I think what turned my heart was learning that he'd kept my book all those years, that it became meaningful to him."

"Your book."

"I wrote it for a laugh. Well, that's not true. I wrote it out of frustration. The mystery of the creative process. I was dealing with my own deep-seated misgivings about the nature of the industry I'd devoted my life to, the nature of the people I strived to impress. It was an outlet and a bit of therapy and a lark, and it got me fired, which was probably the secret reason I'd written it in the first place."

"Because you wrote about Gadsen Wells."

He nodded.

"I wasn't very subtle about it either. I guess I assumed the book would never cross anyone's path. Midwest Hastings had toxified Gadsen Wells twenty years earlier. I came across the internal study that proved it. Of course, the report had been squashed. And I knew our founder, Vlad Chapek, who was still Chairman of the Board, had done it. And in his memoirs, which a few of us chipped in to help write, he didn't even mention Gadsen Wells, like it never happened, like it didn't matter. I hated him for

that. And it's a terrible thing to work for someone or work at something you hate. God, it eats you. Turns you into something small and cruel. I know now that all of that came from inside me, though I told myself at the time I had good reasons to be consumed by bitterness. Chapek was old school in a way you probably can't understand. He didn't want your soul or your life. He didn't care about the people who worked for him, beyond an immediate few, maybe not even them. He didn't care about the communities he affected or the landscape he altered or the betterment of the world. He just wanted his company to grow. Like a cancer, it seemed to me. Like a malignancy."

"So you wrote the novel to tell the story of what happened in Gadsen Wells."

"I wrote it to try and convict Vlad Chapek in the court of bad literature. It was a stupid, futile gesture, but cathartic. I told no one but my first wife. I figured no one would ever see it or connect it to me."

"Grace."

Stoddard waited. "How did you know that?"

"From the inscription inside the cover," I said. "To Grace, love Peter."

He grimaced. And I saw in his expression that he knew a kind of pain that I'd felt.

"Yes," he admitted. "Grace betrayed me, no doubt for very understandable reasons. Neville found the book on her night table, one night when I was travelling on business. And she let him have it, maybe to drive the knife in a little deeper. Nev showed it to Vlad because that's what we do to our

closest friends when we want to hurt them as much as possible, and Vlad showed me the door like I meant nothing to him. I couldn't even find work in North America after that. I had to go to Europe. And when I returned I had different ideas about how to run a company. I named it Chapek so I'd never forget where I'd come from."

He made a gesture, a wave of his hand, nothing grand or pretentious, but it signalled to me, just the same, that he was revealing a world he had created.

"We believe that a corporation should be good in order to do good. We believe that there's profit in pursuing responsible science. That there's an efficient market opportunity to seize in competing on the basis of ethical products and services, that there's an opening to exploit, if you will, the moral failings of other organizations. And we believe that over time, just as the successful strategies of all market leaders get imitated, others will follow our model and a better, more sustainable form of capitalism will be forged as a result and maybe become the norm. There are very few disruptive innovations to the essential American business model. Chapek Energy, or X-Alt if our play goes through, will be one of those disruptions. I'm not being arrogant when I say this but I aim to change the world."

I could not help but remember lying on the bed with Amanda, as she told me about her belief in Chapek.

"So, Samantha wasn't lying to me. She said you were for real. That you were different. Is she working for you now? Or was she working for you all along?"

"We all lie, Frank. We all tell stories. But we shape ourselves and the world in turn by the lies we choose to believe in. I want you to believe in mine."

His smile, sombre but winning, knowing but hopeful. And I admit, though I still hated myself for it in the moment, that a particle of love settled into place within me, a hope for his success, a desire to follow. A need, dare I say it, to contribute.

"Some CEOs are strategists," he continued. "Some are financial wizards. Some are master motivators. I collect good people, some of them lost lambs like yourself, and I put them to work. I want you to work for me. You've been tested in ways few ever experience. It has not been an easy road for you, and I admit, you bring some uncertain qualities and unnervingly combustible"—a nod to my gun—"behaviours. In spite of all that, I can't let you go. I don't want to lose you. I've tracked you for years. Followed your ups and downs. I have this feeling, Frank, a conviction I can't argue myself out of, that you're better than you've ever been, that you have more to offer, that if you throw yourself into a cause with every part of your self, you'll become invested in a new way, immersed in a deep personal contentment, the kind of satisfaction that saints and artists know, and that your life will be richer as a result, and we'll all be enriched by your contribution."

He held out his hand.

"Will you join me? Will you come on board? It doesn't matter what role we find for you. What matters is that you belong."

Have you ever been spoken to like that? By

someone important, weighted with responsibility, who took the time to acknowledge your secret concerns, your misgivings, your dreams, who wanted to heal the hurt within you, and in the same stroke, to pull you past that irresolvable mess, toward something worth pursuing, something noble and honourable, to offer you joy?

I thought of what I'd lost over the years, what I'd been through, how much hurt and loneliness I'd experienced, what a wonder it was that I hadn't killed myself during one of the many dark moments along the way, what a surprise it was that I hadn't lost myself through relinquishment, the letting go of me, the kind of giving up that meant dissolving my struggle for meaning into the compelling rush of external success. How little I'd gained by resisting, and how precious that resistance still seemed. I thought of my promise to Kiedler and Meeks, borne of so much bitterness, to kill the liar who was least convincing. Of the hell I would be consigning myself to in following such a principled stance. Of the torment that such a declaration revealed. Of the relief I felt to know that the security guard was still alive, that Amanda was still alive, that my wife was not with Kiedler. How each story in turn had proved another lie. And yet, Stoddard meant it when he said that we are shaped by lies, that we build the world out of the lies we choose to believe in. This made sense to me in a place and at a depth I had never touched before.

I had only to let go. To reach out. To loosen my hate, my anger, my hurt, and cast it aside, to join Stoddard in something practical but resonant with

eternity, the simple devotion of meaningful work, in the company of like-minded others, in pursuit of something larger than us all. I thought of what that meant, and what it asked of me, and what it said of Stoddard that he'd been able to reach me in such a way. I thought of what I could become. I knew the rules now. I could play within them. I could profit nicely. Not just in a material or financial sense but in terms of compassion. For myself. For others. I could feel respectable. I could be lauded. I could build another life. Get married again. Have a daughter again. Submit myself to the creative act of living well.

I could shoot him. Lift the gun, aim it at his chest and pull the trigger, watch him recoil across the table with the sudden violent shock, hurled there by the force of my hate, and then lay on the onyx surface, his arms spread out, his head turned aside, his eyes closed gently, the watery blood leaking from the hole in his body. Or I could listen and understand.

I felt the gun's weight leave my hand as I released it.

A part of me died as it did so, so part of me might live.

"You still doubt," Stoddard said. "I can tell. You need time to heal. A month or so at Saffron Hills. Then you'll be ready to take on a new role. We all want you. You're an invaluable part of this game that we're playing, a game that we need to win."

His hand was still extended. He did not feel any doubt. He did not waver.

I reached out. His handshake was warm, firm, respectful.

"I'd like that," I said, quietly, as if my hope was too humble to be spoken out loud.

The last of my resistance gave way inside me, and something like faith took over. I knew that I could trust him with every part of myself, my uncertainty, my fears, even my hate. I loved Stoddard in a way I'd never loved anything before.